Para Yani y Carlos:

La Cuba desconocida q'
todos tenemos en el corazón,
país de palabras del q' hay
q' escapar en estampida
para poder quedarnos
para siempre en su
alma.

mi abrazo incesante!

14.2.14

GENERATION ZERO

AN ANTHOLOGY OF NEW CUBAN FICTION

SAMPSONIAWAY.ORG | A PUBLICATION OF CITY OF ASYLUM/PITTSBURGH

Published by Sampsonia Way Magazine,
a publication of City of Asylum/Pittsburgh
324 Sampsonia Way
Pittsburgh, Pennsylvania 15212

www.sampsoniaway.org
www.cityofasylumpittsburgh.org

All facts and characters appearing in this work are fictitious.
Any resemblance to real persons, living or dead, is purely coincidental.

Anthology Editor: Orlando Luis Pardo Lazo
Assistant Editor: Joshua Barnes
Sampsonia Way Managing Editor: Silvia Duarte
Book design: Michael Solano-Mullings

Front cover art by Danilo Maldonado Machado (El Sexto)
Back cover art by Luis Trápaga

Contents

About the Anthology

There are many writers currently creating canon-defying literature inside Cuba. With this in mind, *SampsoniaWay.org* asked its Havana-based Cuban columnist and correspondent Orlando Luis Pardo Lazo to compile a collection of short stories from writers who are creating new trends in Cuban Literature.

For this anthology, Pardo Lazo decided to focus on writers of Generación Año Cero (Generation Year Zero), a movement of writers who began publishing in 2000. He selected 16 short stories from 16 writers and chose to illustrate them with works by the Cuban visual artists Danilo Maldonado, El Sexto, and Luis Trápaga.

Prologue

By Orlando Luis Pardo Lazo
Translated by Mary Jo Porter

New narrative, or *new*rrative, is quite a challenging term. Especially if it comes out of Cuba, a rather claustrophobic island even today, in these post-revolutionary times, when general Raúl Castro is trying to reform most of the social life in order to keep it under his control (including culture and, of course, literature).

As such, Cuban *new*rrative emerges not as a passive reaction but as a creative resistance. It emerges from zero, unexpected, from the very margins of literary tradition and the mainstream, coincidentally starting during the so-called zero years in Cuba: The 2000's decadent decade.

The writers of this *new*rrative do not belong to a single generation, but at some point in their meteoric careers they have called themselves Generation Year Zero. A rather urban phenomenon, interested in prose much more than in poetry, theater, or essay, they have occupied private and public spaces with their performance readings, which include other artistic expressions, such as music and video-clips.

Expelled or self-excluded from several Cuban institutions throughout their peculiar lives, in their texts many of them seem to mutate easily from irreverence to indolence to incredulity to iconoclasm, and are willing to deconstruct all previous discourses of what "cubanness" is supposed to be, whether erotic or political, ultimately betting it all on a kind of cubanless cubanness.

Thus, this *new*rrative comprises a wide range of topics that moves from the sordid, more than dirty realism of Lizabel Mónica and Jhortensia Espineta, to the science fiction of Erick Mota, and the intertextuality of Osdany Morales. Some of these writers even manage to express themselves directly in English (like the music lover Raúl Flores) in a kind of xenophilia that aspires to escape from scholarly Hispanic fundamentalism. Others, such as performance artist Polina Martínez Shviétsova or the translator Abel Fernández-Larrea, try to make music with their prose narratives using a post-Soviet language as if it came from another planet (or from a paleo-Revolution not totally passé, as our rulers are octogenarians who survived the rise and fall of real socialism). There are even writers who appropriate a French learned from watching European film festivals, like the blogger Lia Villares. Some, like Carlos Esquivel and Gleyvis Coro Montanet, give space in their works to a subtle, socially-rooted humor. More than a few are exploring the digital format of the Cuban underground, developing clubs for controversy such as *Espacio Polaroid* (in Havana) and literary and opinion magazines (which are illegal in Cuba) in the style of: *Cacharro(s)* by Jorge Alberto Aguiar Díaz, Lizabel Mónica, and Orlando Luis Pardo Lazo; *33 y 1 tercio* by Raúl Flores, Michel Encinosa, and Jorge Enrique Lage; *The Revolution Evening Post* by Ahmel Echevarría, Jorge Enrique Lage, and Orlando Luis Pardo Lazo; *La Caja de China* by Lien Carrazana; *DesLiz* by Lizabel Mónica; and *Voces* by Orlando Luis Pardo Lazo with the renowned Cuban blogger Yoani Sánchez and her husband, independent journalist Reinaldo Escobar.

This rainbow of e-mergent voices has won almost every national award in Cuba, but it is virtually unheard of outside the island. Some new names have been added to Generation Year Zero (Jamila Medina, Anisley Negrín, Arnaldo Muñoz Viquillón, Legna Rodríguez, and Evelyn Pérez, for example), but they do not appear in this initial anthology, of which *Sampsonia Way Magazine* is now the exclusive publisher. However, the anthology does include the contributions of two controversial graphic artists from Havana: The graffiti artist Danilo Maldonado (otherwise known as "El Sexto") and the painter Luis Trápaga.

We believe that anthologizing, as with translation, is a form of betrayal. To translate an anthology is, therefore, a double betrayal. But, in literature, only the radical positions are the creative ones. All authentic art takes off from disaster and, as we know, language exists because communication is impossible.

We should, then, think of literature literally as heresy; it is never derived from the aesthetics of cultural ecumenism. We should anthologize from anguish and delirium. In literature, pacifism is the worst sin: Every poetic panorama invites violation with a longitudinal cut, which is more effective if we think in terms of opening veins and arteries with every narration. And thus it is that every anthology is always a little prone to suicide (and, equally, to censorship).

All of Cuba behaves so. It is a ghetto of people half-patriotic and half-stateless. A clickless clinic, because in 2013 the government still hasn't authorized its citizens' right to information, which includes, of course, the Internet.

So, to create an anthology in Cuba—a closed fortress placed between internal feudal repression and being the earthly utopia of the international left—is the work of an almost heroic publisher. If, as is the case with this compilation exclusive to *Sampsonia Way Magazine*, we aim to offer the island's emerging literary voices, then we no longer have a simple selection, but rather a bet that forces us to take risks (in numbers, names, topics, and styles). This is a bottle tossed into the future, which can explode like a grenade of infinite meanings or barely return to the reader like a listless boomerang.

Let's be honest: No one knows what will happen tomorrow with the no-longer-that-young Cuban authors of the so-called Generation Year Zero, who are now anthologized from Pittsburgh, or perhaps PittsburgHavana, for the first time in Spanish and English.

Let's even be cynical: It doesn't much matter what happens. Literature and prophecy are not synonymous. There is no guarantee of success beyond the unique universe of each authorial text. Literature does not imply certainty—it's just a symptom of the human experience, which is basically an imaginary experience: Fiction illuminated by emotional memory and expressed according to the limits of language. This is all the wisdom that fits within the literary. And wisdom often ends in dramatic failure.

Let's go even further for once: These authors don't fear that failure. They indefatigably seek it. A successful career is always suspicious, or ends up with the guilty feeling that we are collaborating with the status quo.

No, our anthologized writers do not fit within standardized notions of success. Nor do they fit well within the naive idea of the democratic in the minefields of the literary. In the literary world, the majority tends to be mistaken, asleep between the cliches of the canonical tradition and the miracles of market. A kind of "private public" audience must be conceived again and again by each literary generation—especially if it is a generation of Cubans who seem to avoid the classic concept of the literary field, to provoke a literarid feel, while being held hostage by an obsolete State which aspires to replace them as the Ultimate Narrator.

Thus, between the grandiloquent fictions of Power and the minor literature of the newrrative from the Year Zero, or 2000, Cuban Culture gains nothing or, better yet, gains precisely zero. These writers have become the emptying-out of the author versus the violence of the State. This spontaneous nihilism—which prioritizes the histrionic over the historic, the hedonism of inner exile over revolutionary barbarism, the intimate over the institutional (a residual freedom domestic but undomesticated), and rhetoric over relating—is what this anthology is attempting to photograph: The New Man is not tired of being a committed intellectual; rather, he is tired of being compelled by forces foreign to his own work and will.

In this anthology, the world's readers are now getting a peek at a literature that tries to distance itself from Cuban stereotypes without avoiding the terminal tedium of a day lived to the limit which, for the purposes of these authors, is an endless resistance on the margin of contemporaneity.

The Sky Over Havana

Story by Jorge Alberto Aguiar Díaz

Translated by Zachary A. Tackett

"

I'm dying, damn it, and you're going to die alone on this shitty island!" she shouted at him.

Then she hit him. Violently. It split open his lips and nose. It left him collapsed against the wall.

"Tell me, faggot, why don't you hit me back?"

She spat on him. He became still. Looked up. Then he saw the sea. Dawn.

She talked about her money. He wanted to go down to the reefs. Get his feet wet, wash off the blood. She talked about the honeymoon in Japan, about the permanent visa to the United States, about dual citizenship, about her rich and powerful family in Venezuela. He wanted to get his feet wet. To sleep. Maybe even sleep under the water, in another world.

A policeman walked up the sidewalk across the street. He stood waiting. She saw him.

"What if I were to say that you were hurting me? What do you think about that? What can happen to you for conning and taking advantage of a tourist?"

He also saw the policeman. A second. He looked at the sea again. What would happen then? A starving Cuban and a tourist from the First World. Who would believe him? And when the police asked why she attacked? What could he say? The real answer was so unlikely that it would get him locked up in a prison cell. He leaned against the wall. In the distance he heard a ship announcing its entry into the bay. The policeman remained on the sidewalk. She attacked me because she wants me to marry her and go back to her country, he would answer. "And I do not want to," he thought. Everyone was going to taunt him, the police and his friends, when they heard. His wife and his mistress, of course, they wouldn't believe anything.

"Tell me. What if I call the police?"

He did not answer. He was breathing anxiously and with some difficulty. I forgive you, Ana Marina, he thought. He recalled her naked, moaning with pleasure. Always laughing. He recalled her long, beautiful, black hair. He turned his face to see her one last time. Stunning and pallid. With her hair swept up under a scarf.

"It's all the same to me," he said. "If you want to, kill me. I am free, Ana Marina, free."

Before closing his eyes, he heard a seagull in the distance and smiled.

He woke up. Once again the view of the sea from his window in that little room in Malecón. A piece of sea and a window. He had nothing else. A dirty mattress, a typewriter, a few pesos to buy rum and get drunk. He thought of Ana Marina. She would arrive from London at noon at the latest. But at least he was going to eat well for a week. He also needed to get out of this slum filled with prostitutes and criminals.

He looked at the blank page. Not a word. To write is to destroy oneself. He stood up. He had to forget his hopes of being a writer. He looked down the avenue—still deserted at dawn. He yawned. Hunger. Tiredness. Ennui. The entire early morning to write at least one page. No novel, no money, and no hope. What could he do? Wait. But wait for what? Nothing. Only wait. Waiting is enough. He thought of Ricardito, of Kimani, of El Bolo. His friends were determined. That night they would launch into the sea on a raft. Such an irony. Some arriving by plane in first class and others escaping in rustic rafts.

A shout threw him out of his tired state. It was the

neighbor. Once again fighting with her husband. Every day, the man arrived from the street at this hour and beat her. A mulatto ex-convict who made her whore for a dollar at the corner of Monte and Cienfuegos. Why not write those stories that he saw every day? Why not write about his rafting friends? Why not write about Ana Marina?

He took out the letters he had sent to her in the last six months. He wanted to reread them. Something was wrong. He never spoke of leaving the country. She, however, had phoned him three days before to say: I'll come get you. We will get married, and I will get you out of Cuba in less than a month. I love you.

He looked at the letters. He recalled her naked. He remembered her beautiful, long hair. He thought he would like to make love to her in the middle of the city, behind the wall of the Malecón, on the reefs. But this marriage and escape puzzled him. What about his wife? And his lover?

He opened a letter. He began to read. In the distance, he heard the siren of a ship.

They had met on Obispo Street. She had gone to a bookstore looking for the books of Carpentier, Lezama, and Reinaldo Arenas. They had discussed literature. They had talked about their lives. No timidity, no hypocrisy, no repression, no guilt. They had liked each other at first sight. An hour later they were thinking that they had known each other all their lives. She got too drunk, and he loved her voluptuous body, her hair, her way of speaking, her age. "I go crazy for both young and mature women," he confessed. She had turned forty-five, ten years his senior. He spoke then of his wife who was nearly fifty and his lover of eighteen. The flower and the fruit of life.

Ana Marina invited him to a bottle of rum. She lived every moment as if it was her last. "You are a person sick of words and I am sick of life," she said walking down Obispo, searching for the sea and Plaza de Armas.

The dealers offered them everything. Cigars, inexpensive luxurious food, rum, aphrodisiacs. Anywhere you could go, a huge black man showed up, selling any good, suggesting women, grabbing his own balls. They walked slowly, seeing everything and talking about what we always talk about: Government, human rights, the difficulties of traveling abroad, poverty, hunger, child prostitution.

The heat made them both sweat and her nipples were visible through her shirt. She put her hand under her shirt to dry them and he wanted to bite her there, like an animal, and pounce on top of her. Ana Marina's eyes looked with longing, discovered an untamed instinct. "I would like to dry off your sweat," he said as they sat in the park. "And I would like you to dry me off," she said.

That night was spent in the small room in Malecón. They endured the heat, the bad smell and the filth of the overflowing toilet in the middle of the slum's hallway, the shouts and fights of neighbors over a lack of water. He opened the windows and entered her forcefully. He grabbed her by the waist, bit her back and they looked out at the sea. In the distance, they heard a seagull and a ship announcing its arrival to Havana.

The policeman crossed the street.

She was crying and questioning herself. Life is shit. Why do we live like we live? The worst fear is not of death but of life.

He was also crying. He had spoken of his freedom. He had spoken of writing, of self-destruction, of the love for his wife and his lover.

"Well, aren't you just a tropical playboy! You piece of shit! How can you love two women, huh? Egotist. You only love yourself."

The police stopped again five or six meters away. She had her back turned.

"Why the fuck did you promise to marry me? Why the

fuck did I come to this island of shit? Narcissist! Fucking playboy!"

She wanted to hit him again. She understood it was useless. He looked like a mangy dog leaning against the wall, swallowing blood and his fear of living.

"You're not worth anything. You have wasted the opportunity of a lifetime. Stupid. Failure. You will never even amount to a mediocre writer."

And that's how she went. She barely watched the traffic as she crossed the street. The cop walked away smiling.

He was alone. He listened to the waves. It was daylight.

Ana Marina, Havana is a village. And since you left, Havana is like a ghost town. I think of you every day. No exaggeration. If we had not met in that bookstore, we would be missing something. Something that we would need. You are real and you are a ghost. All I have left is language. And language names the impossible, an absence that time reconstructs in our imagination in order to escape death. So my words condemn me to live in the solitude of my own loneliness. Enclosed in this tiny room, I look at the sea. I live paying rent that I can no longer afford, but I need to be alone. I want to write. I can not live without writing. I see my wife and my girlfriend two or three times a week; sometimes they are tolerant of my loneliness. If they did not exist, I wouldn't think twice about marrying you. Since you left, you are the ghost; the smell of these sheets materializes in infinite desire, in pleasure that is already pain and forgetfulness. You live in love because you are pure instinct. A force that destroys to create. I am adrift in this adrift city. I don't want to live if it's not to write and be with both of those women, with those two women who I need so much and who resembled happiness. And here you come. I am afraid. Sometimes I think I'll die before I'm forty. Is this possible? I need time. I'm lost inside myself.

He put the letter aside. Ana Marina was about to arrive at any moment. Six months later she is returning. Six months later he is still there, living in the same disgusting mansion in ruins, sitting with his head in his hands, waiting. Waiting for what? Just waiting. Waiting —period.

He looked at the sea. He saved all of the letters. They all said the same. The same ideas in different words. He thought of his friends. He thought of his lover and his wife.

They left the Plaza de Armas and walked again toward Obispo. She invited him to her hotel. He said no and told her of his little room. They spent the last two days touring the city and always ended in that cavern. Three hours before her departure they were still there. What could they do? Say goodbye.

She would return a second time. He wrote a poem for her. A breeze entered through the window and cooled the heat. They had lived a shameless freedom without any consequences, they had unleashed their ghosts. They lived all the fantasies they ever wanted to live. To feel the impulse of death behind every minute. To transfigure life into something that is not a thing, a simplification of the absurd, a stultifying routine, a connection to the Machine, he wrote to her.

I like your poem. And I like your hair. Would you like to leave Cuba? Yes, but not to stay. Why? I have to write. You are so strange. Yes, and I'm crazy and whatever you want, but I have to write. Sentenced to write in this light that blinds me. Do you feel free? Sure. After all, one day you discover that freedom is hidden in your head. Is freedom for you to be with two women at the same time? Why do you ask that? Don't you think you're falling into a cliché? Forgive me, it's that I was jealous. Jealous? Yes, jealous. You're falling in love. It is possible, and I know it will be hard to forget you. You will forget me. No. Yes. I'll never forget you. Neither will I.

"Y-you going w-with us or are you st-st-staying?" Ricardito asked.

"Let's go, man, this place is shit. There's no future here, said El Bolo."

Kimani did not speak. Kimani always spoke very little. One night he said it all, and then never spoke of the matter again: We have to get out. Cuba is not a real place. Cuba does not exist.

They were in the door of his slum. Everything was ready. The raft, canned meat, medicines, compass. Everything.

"I have to stay. Maybe in a year or two …"

"Are you crazy, man! You said that two years ago."

"Are y-you sc-scared?"

He did not answer. So many questions to answer!

He checked his watch. Ana Marina was coming. His friends planned their death and he was there waiting. A corpse that sees how the others will die.

"K-Kimani, s-say something."

Kimani was going to say something, but he stifled himself. Suddenly, the wife of the ex-convict fell into a ball in the hallway of the house. The black man came up behind her and hit her right there with a hose. He gave two or three kicks and left her unconscious.

Some neighbors intervened. The guy came out of the lot, crossed the street and sat on the wall of the Malecón.

"Let's go guys," Kimani said.

Five minutes after his friends were gone, a Panataxi arrived and Ana Marina stepped out. He saw her from the window. Then he looked up. He stared at the horizon.

Finally he went down to the reefs. He wiped off the blood. The water was cold. She was right. He was an idiot. He would never be even a mediocre writer. His wife was about to leave him. She knew about his lover and eventually she would break up with him. The young one, with her mere eighteen years, needed life, and he was vegetating.

The future had become an idea. A single idea. Stay and wait. So just wait. He sat on a rock. He dipped his feet. Freedom could be inside one's head, but he put his head under water anyway. To live in another world. To be a seagull, the whistle of a ship.

He thought of his friends. When he couldn't hold his breath any longer, he flung his head out. He inhaled the breeze. It was beginning to get hot. He heard the noises of the city.

She got out of the Panataxi. Two guys, one giant white man and one black man with huge gold chains, approached her to offer her something. Everything a foreigner needs to be happy in the largest of the Antilles. She looked at the window. She looked at the gate. She saw an old man sleeping in a doorway, some children came to her asking for candy, two children who went tourist hunting from early on.

She closed the door of the taxi. She paid. Gave him a tip.

She entered smiling at the slum. Where is my great writer? Where is my tropical man? She stopped at the door. The wife of the ex-convict had recovered and came out with a knife in hand looking for the husband. An old woman, indifferent to everything that had happened, threw stew at her pig and corn at her chickens.

The toilet was overflowing. Someone had the record player blaring. And in another room, someone was listening to a speech by Fidel on the radio. Ana Marina smiled. She knocked on the door a second time.

Ana Marina, as Virgilio Piñera said, one day you will see that I was right to stay and live in my country. Logic and a sense of history. What else do you need to know? The sense of history can be the sense of a country but also, and above all it should be, the sense of a human being. It is possible to love two women. Even three. True love is not possession. Cuba does not exist. The world does not exist. My rebellion is pointless. Nor is it to live domesticated. Should I end in suicide? No. I wait. What do I wait for? Nothing. Only wait.　　*nihilism*

He stopped writing. He left the paper on the table. She would read it after she arrived from the airport. He sat down to wait for his friends. They would come to confirm their trip for that night.

He prayed that they would not see Ana Marina arrive. "Fairy Godmother" as Kimani called her when he told Kimani that she was daddy's little girl and that she had a lot of money and lived in London.

But she will not pay attention to those words. Language is death itself. She would live a week with him. They would make love again with the same passion and freedom. In a hotel, in the small room of the slum, near the reefs. One week. Enough time for a decision.

"Everything is decided. I told you that I don't want to leave."

"Don't tell me that. You have a week to make up your mind."

"Everything is decided."

"No, please. I'll come get you. I'm dying."

"We are all dying."

"I'm dying," she would say.

And she will undress. He'll be on his back watching the sea and will not see her nakedness until she calls him, tells him, "look at me," and then will turn slowly to look at her. And he will look at her.

"I'm dying," she will say a second time.

He will see an unknown body. A black spot, a breast amputated. And he will understand. Understand why she took off her clothes, why she came with her long, beautiful black

25

hair tied in a handkerchief. Why it is no longer black nor long nor beautiful, of the cancer that progresses, that eats her voluptuous body, of chemotherapy, of the pain.

"Let's live together for what I have left."

"Ana Marina, we are lost among such fear and such loneliness."

He would watch the sea. Like a corpse that sees the death of the entire universe.

"I love you."

"I love you too, but it can't be."

Kimani is alone on the open sea. He closes his eyes. He doesn't want to see so much darkness all around him.

Graphomania

Story by Lien Carrazana Lau

Translated by Maria Lourdes Capote

I heard your voice through a photograph
I thought it up, it brought up the past
Once you know you can never go back
I've got to take it on the other side.

—*"Otherside,"* Red Hot Chili Peppers

It's Sunday. Exactly eleven eleven when you first kiss me.

"Good morning, honey. Good morning, my love." We stay like this a while, wrapped in the bed covers, with the tenuous light of a day much too gray and cold to be a Sunday in Havana.

We eat breakfast. As strange as it seems, it's you who makes the coffee. I open the window and Havana's winter displays its beauty before our eyes.

We go out dressed as if we were in Europe and these were not our only elegant winter coats. You carry your Nikon with new ammunition: An entire roll just for us, to squander at La Cabaña while we stroll through the fair, look at books, inspect the bookshelves, greet everyone we know, and ask anyone: "Could you take our picture?"

We take our picture on the wall that stretches before us as we contemplate Havana from above. We feel superior being above a sea of people that passes by on the streets below. We drink a beer while we look at the sea, and when a vessel appears at the perfect time, we make plans over the plans that we had already made.

I smile for your lens; the wind musses my hair, which I am growing longer to please you. I am trying to ignore the superstition that every time I let my hair grow something happens, something ends or turns out badly. I look at my hair. It is shoulder length already, and some of that disjointed fear comes back, but I prefer to believe that this time it will be different.

I buy a small book of sonnets. I harbor a secret hope that I will scrutinize the author in his words and peel back that false veil that we put between ourselves and others. I stop by the author's table to get his autograph. You greet him; he is someone you've known for a long time. You introduce me as your girlfriend, your longtime girlfriend. This always makes me feel young, yet sometimes I have trouble imagining being introduced as your girlfriend four years from now, with a child in a baby carriage, but right now there's no child and no baby carriage, nor have four years passed by.

The sun begins to set (as they say in poorly written stories), but to us it seems a logical shift towards nightfall. We return to the large mass of cement. I see the tunnel's lights, orange and expectant, and it's like returning to the maternal womb, like opening my eyes right now to find that I have traveled from this recliner and, without opening my eyes, continue traveling to the exact point at which opening my eyes will mean tears.

Warm tears flow from my eyes, allowing themselves to trickle with desires which vanish with the light that brings me back to this tacit room, filled with photographs scattered all over the floor. But I know that opening my eyes and crying will be part of the process of imagining everything, absolutely everything, and I wouldn't be able to cry again, I wouldn't need to cry since I have already done so in my mind.

You are right: Writing is useless; it is a repetition of that which you have already done with your thoughts. That is why you do not write. Is it better to leave everything to the imagination and to life itself?

I don't know. I contradict my own thoughts. I attack these pages with my graphomania, I prostitute my sleep into a vigil, and I transport it to these cells covered with words. I, and only I, am responsible for my life, the life that no one wrote for me and that is why it's so difficult to act out some makeshift role.

Perhaps I was born cursed. But no, I don't think so. We don't have executioners, curses, wars that depend on us. We are not children struggling for a crown. We are only dust in the wind, just like melody coming from the radio, when everything is extremely calm outside, and yes, I do feel like dust in the wind, dust that floats in a spiral over this island.

I am just another young girl, scribbling ideas in a notebook bought for 3.05 CUC (a currency easy to exchange with shit, just like colonial payments). Yesterday, in a post-orgasm haze you said, I said, we both said: "I don't want to live a fictional life, to buy make-believe food with make-believe money in a make-believe store."

But the reality is, that fictional or real, life leaves its traces on us. The head begins turning grey, hair falls out and we are here, inside this room, where the savage clarity brought on before orgasm brings music and hostile shadows to my mind. For me, many Cubas exist. For you, there's only one. In reality, there's only one. This hot country, peopled with workers and vagabonds, with altruistic men and despots, with writers and waitresses, with hangers-on and teachers, with violators and men who follow the law, with pioneers and foreigners. The Cuba of the Festival and the Arts, the revolutionary myth, the terrestrial dinosaur, a seawall that traces borders around my ideas, but again I am mistaken, you are right, only one Cuba exists.

All the Cubas I see with each eye are nothing more than a subtle trap in this fictional game. I am assuming this; I was born surrounded by portraits of illustrious men. I am an unbreakable doll. "Take me; do with me whatever you want, indoctrinate me, give me a destiny, a death, an ideology..." This was written upon my forehead from the beginning.

I get comfortable in the recliner and grab a handful of photographs. Yellowed photographs. My Chinese grandfather in a visa-sized photo. I read the back: Taken August

10th, 1958. This is the only image I have of my grandfather. I never knew him; all I have is this photo. His face is long and serious. His eyes are sad, nostalgic, questioning.

I look for a visa-sized picture of me. I look at my face and for the first time I realize that I resemble him. Something deep in my eyes is also found deep in his eyes. My smile is crooked on the left side, just like his. Maybe, against all predictions, I could be the one that looks most like him in our family. Like that inscrutable Chinese man that landed on our island when he was only 18, and changed his un-pronounceable name to the more western Jose, that man whose Asian last name my offspring will not inherit, just like they will not inherit his/my smile or that mystery that no one will know in its entirety: Our I, our real name that we carry inside like a treasure that can never be usurped.

Gray photos. Pictures of my mother's fifteenth birthday party, a huge table full of sweets, sodas, an enormous cake, a group of boys and girls around my mother at the center of the composition. My mother: An adolescent girl with short hair, a necklace made from seeds, and the clothing of some-one engaged in the Literacy Campaign. My mother: a young woman of her time, the future of the nation.

I don't have any photos of my fifteenth birthday cele-bration. I didn't care for rented long dresses, or the poses. On my fifteenth birthday there was no costume as authen-tic as my mother's had been. Cuba was already a country free from illiteracy and turning fifteen meant nothing like before when you were "presented to society." The nation was immovable like a turtle asleep in the Caribbean.

Color photos. My lyrical years: The beginning of my youth, my innocent years. A picture of me at twenty. Varadero Beach. On the sand is written the word: LONELI-NESS. The beach is perfect: The water transparent, the sky an impeccable blue, the sand finer than salt. But I was alone; you were not on the other side of the lens like you are now, looking at me sitting in this recliner, surrounded by photos, with the window open to a gray and familiar Havana.

"You enjoy constructing catastrophes," you say with a smile. I like stirring up the past. Once I tried using one of the photos as a portal to return there, but that is no longer possible, I am outside of everything. I live in this consciousness, at the end of the lyrical age. And it is much better like that.

The red recliner is my own private island. From my shore I see you on the other side of the lens; from my recliner-island I am like a shipwrecked person waving her little flag in the direction of your ship. You blink like the flash of the Nikon. My photo watches you waiting for the morning coffee, the winter that does not exist in this tropical Havana, going together to the fair. The photos that we do not have. "I only have black and white rolls, honey; besides, look how sunny it is today, you know what the fair must be like on a Sunday," you say and your ship retreats, leaving me for the computer.

I go out. Squeezed by these four walls, I am unable to breathe. Mud walls full of holes that filter sounds, water, restlessness. I can't find peace. Peace doesn't exist outside, in any place where I am now. A stream of people moves over its absence. I am sad. My sadness is a downpour falling on these people, the words bouncing in my brain. It is the city in pieces, asphyxiated, agonizing in amnesia. I scream inside, but my voice is extinguished in my guts.

I walk with the crowd. The Book Fair, words fair, thoughts fair. People buy bread, beer. They smoke, fall in love, stand in line, smile, dance, recite poetry, take pictures by the seawall with Havana in the background. Among them I walk. I walk as if I were a transparent woman. Each drop of water pierces me and dissolves part of me into the sea, into the air, into the black earth, into the faces, into the footsteps, into the amorphous body of the multitude.

A book. I want to find a book among the many. It would be like finding a gem we believed to be extinct. I remember the presentation for the book of sonnets. The author has a Jewish last name, a magical profile, and wears his shirts tucked in. I didn't like the sonnets. They fail to bring me to the other side. I left the book on the table where the author was signing them.

I walk from one pavilion to another. In olden times it was a prison for bodies, today a prison for words. I don't find anything, only writers and readers gathered in each corner of Cabaña Fortress. There's only a precipice. I sit at the edge and imagine my body falling and getting squashed in the grass below. In the very spot where they shot someone who also wanted to, one day, find a book that would save his life. Perhaps he found it, and because of that book he decided to die.

I return to the city. It is raining. Down Obispo Street, the same strip full of legs, arms, shoulders, hips: The crowd under the cold February rain. My tears mix with the rain like a theatre curtain that hides my sadness. But nobody notices. I can cry in front of everyone because nobody sees me. I am dissolved into the evening, the cobblestones, the umbrellas.

I turn right on Havana Street. The Belen district. The black neighborhood, a poor area, my neighborhood. I walk down my street. Music submerges my ears in an inescapable sentence. The reggaeton of my neighbor on the corner returns me to my habitat. The rainwater makes the odors of dried flowers and the rotten food in the garbage cans seem more pungent. Mud reaches my feet. I am a lotus flower again.

I go up the stairs. My anguish diminishes with each step up. "Otherside" can be heard through the door; the music of the Red Hot Chili Peppers brings me back to you. Inside it's hotter than hell. You sweat in front of the fan as you clean your camera's lens. "Did you buy a book?" you ask, looking at my wet hair falling over my shoulders.

I don't answer. I smile at you and go inside the bathroom. For an instant my eyes scrutinize the other I in the mirror. I look at myself wanting to enter, to fuse with, to penetrate the center of my being. Return to myself. I leave the bathroom. I sit at the computer: "There is no better place than oneself."

I start typing so I can find this book that I need to find. Tomorrow will be Monday and the Book Fair will close. Tomorrow I will cut my hair so that nothing bad happens with us. I will buy a roll of color film. I want to see the city from the lighthouse; I will ask you to take me to El Morro Castle, the phallus of this hermaphroditic Havana, a lit Habano cigar going around in circles looking for penetration. "Penetrate me, stranger," whispers Havana the whore from her vaginal harbor.

I will spread my legs so that your lens will coagulate me along with him/her (Habano/Havana) and we all remain forever caught in the memory. Tomorrow the umbilical cord that ties me to this recliner and to this, my fiction, and to my death from words, will break. Tomorrow I will have my freedom stamped in a passport and my grandfather's smile upon my lips. Because tomorrow, my love, today's time will be over.

Hating Summer

Story by Gleyvis Coro Montanet

Translated by Karen González

" You messed up the form," said the officer as he offered them a new sheet. "You wrote 'climatic' and this is a survey of just checking the boxes, it does not admit handwriting."

"But we are asking for asylum due to climatic reasons," replied the man.

"The choices are 'economic' or 'political.' Nobody asks for asylum due to climatic motives."

"We do," insisted the man. "We hate the summer heat."

"We don't grant asylum for hating the summer heat."

"Why?"

"It's not a serious reason."

"And what's a serious reason?"

"The political and economic causes listed in the form."

The man scratched his head. He looked at his wife.

"But it's a very narrow question, if at least there were a few lines where we could explain..."

"I already told you that it's a survey of just checking the boxes," replied the upset officer. "If you're going to mess it up again, you'd better give it back to me. We're running low on forms."

The man and the woman looked at each other sadly.

"Listen," intervened the officer, "just check any of the two boxes and that's it, don't be a fool."

"You think so?"

"Of course I think so." The officer put his mouth near the opening in the crystal window. He made a mysterious sign, as if asking them to get closer too, from their side, to the crystal in the cabin. "What is the real reason you're asking for asylum?"

"Because we hate the heat of the summer," insisted the man; he then took a pencil, looked at his wife. "You tell me, dear: What reasons are closer to our hatred of the heat, political or economic?"

"Check political," she suggested. "It must be the government's fault."

"It could also be due to the economy."

"Yes, it could," she agreed.

"No," the man was fed up. "The right thing to say is 'climatic.'"

And he wrote again: "climatic".

"Here you go."

"But...are you stupid?!" the officer crumpled the form.

The man tried to raise his fist, but the woman stopped him in time.

"Leave it," she said. "Stuck in this cabin and with that uniform, he is probably more upset by the heat than we are."

A Message for Grethel

Story by Ahmel Echevarría Peré

Translated by Zachary A. Tackett

We met at the Cinematheque. We had taken the same bus and watched the city though the small window without trying to talk. In truth, I watched her when she wasn't looking. At the theatre I noticed her in line behind me. There was a smile, and another ten minutes of waiting to buy a ticket. I realized when it came time to pay that I only had four coins worth 20 cents and a peso in my pockets. I had forgotten my wallet at home.

I looked through my pockets again: Keys, a peso, coins, and the bus fare bulletin. Nothing else. The ticket clerk was impatient with my delay. As the line grew longer he got angry.

I cursed.

"Two, please," she said to the ticket clerk and looked back at me. "Today is my turn to pay. Did you forget?"

She gave me a wink. I wanted to go along with her game, but I couldn't find the words.

She smiled.

I thanked her.

The employee muttered again.

We walked into the movie.

From my seat, I saw her choose her own seat a few rows away. She put on her headphones. She was listening to her Walkman until the lights went down. No one sat next to her.

I left for the lobby before the final credits, feeling ridiculous. The entire way to our seats I had only said a stupid "thank you." I needed to see her, apologize, make up some story in the hope that I could appear less stupid to her. I was so worried I could barely pay attention to the movie.

I didn't have time to invent some excuse. She came out to the lobby right away. I walked toward her. "Excuse me, I don't even know your name, and I'm in debt to you."

I suggested we meet up some other time. She smiled. She said that it'd be pointless to meet up again if I forgot my wallet.

"Putting it in my pocket wouldn't help me much. Do you have a pen?"

Then I wrote my number on the back of the bulletin that I always carried in my pocket.

She looked into her purse, ripped a page from her agenda, and wrote something.

"When you call, say that it's for me and leave a message. I don't like to bother my neighbor."

In addition to her neighbor's phone number Grethel also gave me her email address.

She didn't have a telephone in her house, and I was only able to look at my messages two times a week at a computer lab for writers and artists. To top it all off, we were going in opposite directions.

She was in a hurry. She apologized. She was going to visit a "Patricia" and couldn't change her plans. The night seemed promising. No one was as used to so many setbacks as me. I had a list of such setbacks, an endless list.

I decided to walk her to the bus stop. We ran. The bus was about to leave. As we ran, I asked her if we could see each other the following day, and proposed that we meet at the Cinematheque at 8 pm. Grethel, before boarding the bus, searched in her purse, took out a twenty-peso bill and said, "Here. If we're going to see each other tomorrow, you need to get back to your house first."

I had met a woman and in less than five hours I owed her money. I figured that my life was about to change again.

Was this a good sign? I need setbacks to know that something is going well. If not, it's not worth expending the energy.

We met up again at the Cinematheque the following day. She didn't accept the money when I tried to pay her back, but she did agree to pay me a visit.

It wasn't the last time we saw each other.

In a little more than ten months we had seen every corner of the city. Theaters, museums, movies, the seawall, both her and my friends, parties; one time I even went to church with her, and then I promised to go to the doctor with her, but she just didn't want to talk about it much.

We weren't doing badly and I wanted to ask her to move into my apartment. If it didn't work, she could move back to her house.

I knew that I needed time, quiet, and space for my projects. I wanted to write, take photos, and draw. It was too much, but I was euphoric. More than having the desire to go out and conquer women, I preferred to share my euphoria and space with Grethel.

I guess the closest feeling to having met her is winning the lottery.

But we are no longer even.

I wrote her a note. It was a short message, only half a page, but I needed the whole night to write it. Coffee, music, writing, crossing out whole paragraphs, more coffee, standing on my balcony facing a sleeping city.

I repeated the cycle until exhaustion. I managed to finish the note at the break of dawn.

albahaca_75@yahoo.es

Perhaps her mailbox is the only possible place for a new meeting.

The last time we saw each other face to face was in

my apartment. It was almost noon. She was wearing casual clothing, her hair in pigtails, her lovely big eyes brighter than everything, carrying a backpack, and two completely full bags. The day before, she had called me in the afternoon:

"My Saturday's free, I'd like to stop by your house. Can you set aside your work for a moment?"

I was obsessed with the writing of a collection that barely differed from the structure of a diary and with a series of paintings of which I only had the sketches for a pair of works. I felt a sense of grace passing more time than usual in front of my computer, the block of notes, or my sketchbook. But in reality I was exhausted and I accepted Grethel's proposal. A Saturday with her could help me relax. No books, no computers, no brushes, no tempera. Maybe just some notes.

I told her yes.

Then, she asked me if I could also give her Sunday.

"I can't say no; you're the most awful woman in the world. By the way, weren't we going to go to your consultation this week?"

"I need to talk to you. It's very important."

Our relationship was going smoothly, and I thought that the conversation would be about us moving in together.

"I'll bring food and beer. Saturday will be a special day and I want to celebrate."

To Grethel, Saturday would be a special day but her suggestion caught me by surprise. I was faced with another setback; I had forgotten something. I have a poor memory for dates and names, which Grethel knows well. I was convinced that I had not forgotten her birthday. It was still one week away.

For Grethel, my silence was enough.

"Don't worry. But I don't know whether I should hold you at gunpoint to remember dates or just get used to your poor memory."

"Did I ever tell you that I won the lottery when I met you?"

"Hundreds of times, but it's not enough—I want to hear something more."

I didn't dare ask what I had forgotten. I went back to apologizing and she said, "It will pass. I've become a silly girl, corny, maybe because of my music collection."

It could be truly dangerous for Grethel to have her recordings on hand. Her collection of blues, boleros, and "feeling" was a mix more lethal than cancer, according to her. She'd put the CDs in and, most of the time, she'd end up depressed and without the energy to do anything, except listen to them again. One after another. Until pain.

"Give them away or throw them away, please just get rid of them."

"There's no going back. Call it metastasis. Now I am also a dumb girl addicted to those CDs."

I interrupted her.

I told her that she had gone mad.

She paused before responding.

"Pay no attention to me. Certainly, we're going to celebrate this Saturday our 11-month anniversary, and with grandeur; we deserve it. I promise it won't end like the last time we did it."

I was right; she had gone mad. It was a dreadful celebration. Grethel arrived at my apartment complaining of stabbing pains in her breast. It didn't disappear as night fell. I wanted to take her to the hospital, but she said it was nothing. I insisted; she lost control. We argued. We wanted to celebrate, but the day ended with a fight. I left her alone with her music collection. I left for my studio. I turned on the computer and tried to work on my *Cuaderno de Altahabana*.

I wasn't able to concentrate. I tried my brushes and tempera. I left it all, and decided to make coffee, hoping that the infusion could calm us down and make peace.

After taking a cup of coffee to her, I sat on the bed. I couldn't stop looking at Grethel. Lying there, naked, her hair wild, and those eyes red with tears. When we aren't tumbling, I imagine her as a toy. A tender toy.

I couldn't stop looking at her. I suspected that Grethel was the best thing that had happened to me in years.

I told her.

Big mistake.

Grethel got up, pulled the sheet.

I followed her.

"Get off of me."

"What is it?"

"I suppose that I am upset about you "suspecting"… That's not what I wanted to hear, but it's something. At least it's something. I'm confused… I'm confused and I don't know what to do. To make matters worse, I have this damn pain."

I tried to pet her.

She refused.

"Why don't we go see a doctor?"

"It's nothing. You know what? I'm afraid. I don't know what they could tell me."

"But what do you have to fear?"

"I guess I'm afraid of the words… Nor do I know if I would have preferred to hear a phrase as silly as 'I love you.' Do you think it's a silly phrase? However, I would have liked to hear it. I can look silly or corny, I don't care, I'm not at all modern."

"You messed it all up."

I asked her if she had ever tried to tell someone that she loved him.

She wiped her tears and said she needed to rest.

Grethel: A model to assemble. At each meeting I held in my hands a new part. I was looking for the place to put it. I wanted to have all the pieces. I wanted to put them all together.

"Get off of me."

She left the room and went to the bathroom.

In our country, is it impossible to say 'I love you'? Nobody ever told me. And in that phone conversation I mentioned it to Grethel: "Here, nobody is able to say 'I love you', no one says so. Can't we say it at all...? I haven't figured this out."

And in her call, she reminded me that she was not a modern girl and that I owed her a phrase.

"You stayed silent. Don't mind me... For God's sake, say something."

"Ever wonder why nobody in this country can say 'I love you'? We should find the answer. Will you help me?"

"I suppose I also need to know why."

We said goodbye.

Before hanging up, she said that it would be good for us to meet:

"I'm such a fool that I always forgive your bad memory."

After the call with Grethel, I went out and spent half of my money for the month. I returned with vegetables, fruits, a bottle of wine, cheese, and ham. Everything for her, except half the cheese and ham.

Now I only had to wait for her.

We would have a small feast.

When I opened the door, she smiled. Asked for help. She was carrying two heavy bags and a backpack. Sweating. I had never seen her hair in those pigtails.

I put the bags and backpack on the floor. I took her hands. I looked at her.

"What are you doing?" she said.

I kissed her. Long, deep. Kissed her chin and breasts. With a gentle gesture she tried to stop me.

"Does it hurt?"

"It's nothing, but I'm dirty."

I kept on kissing.

"Someone could see us," she gently removed from my mouth the small crucifix and part of the gold chain she hung it on.

We entered the apartment.

Grethel went to the bathroom while I went to the kitchen. I unpacked. While she was bathing, I asked if she had gone to the doctor and she said that she had come prepared to spend several days with me: "That's why I bought food and beer. I also brought some music."

I opened her bag and crossed my fingers. Inside was the case with her favorite albums.

"Will you forget about your projects at least for this weekend?"

We had been together eleven months, and what Grethel had bought appeared to be to celebrate a real anniversary. I thought about telling her, but I decided to stay quiet.

I heard the water falling in the shower as I cut the cheese and ham. Grethel was singing. I finished preparing the dish with crackers and olives, and poured two glasses of red wine.

As I opened the bathroom door, Grethel was beginning to lather. I pulled on her pigtails.

"I have a surprise," I kissed her neck and gently bit her ear. By the way, didn't we have to talk?

"Today, we will celebrate."

I took everything to the living room. On a tablecloth on the floor I set dishes, glasses, the bottle of wine, and two incense sticks.

I turned on the TV. The news had just begun. This was truly a master class: Pure action from start to finish, digressions between each scene; two stories told in unison and only one of them travels on the airwaves. An immense iceberg fired accurately from the cathode ray tube.

Grethel left the bathroom. She smelled of violets, and

the world promised to be in one of its worst moments. She sat next to me. The newscaster started talking about the national elections, and Grethel wanted to let her hair down.

"Stay like this. You look like a teenager; you appear to be fifteen."

"That young?"

And I went to kiss her again.

My heart was about to collapse, and her cheeks were flushed. I put her hand on my chest, she put mine on her chest and then on her lips. She bit my fingers gently, hugged me. Very quietly said "Then I'll be a girl."

She fixed her pigtails and started kissing my cheeks, my neck, my lips.

I took a piece of ham and a piece of cheese. A bite for both.

Grethel stood before me with her back to the TV. I undressed her slowly. First the sweater, very slowly. Then I kissed her navel, her belly, her breasts, and there was a slight sigh when I touched her neck with my lips. I undressed her slowly. I pulled down the legs of her sweatpants to leave her legs bare. All her skin bristled with the touch of my fingers. I looked at her face, her body. Only one piece of lace remained. Black. Minimal. I put my fingers in the elastic, slowly, watching every detail of her body as I pulled, very carefully, much like a rescue team pulling from between the rubble some bodies crushed and some alive. There were images of an earthquake. Indonesia, 8.7 on the Richter Scale. The city was under the rubble. A violent shaking came from Grethel. She removed my sweater, straddled me, and stopped being that teenager like a tender toy. Nothing further from a little girl. Just take all her pieces, change their places, and you'll have another Grethel.

I started to drive into her with my penis. Hard, under my jean shorts. And she looked at me. Smiled, slightly. I kissed her lips, her breasts. And reached for the glasses of wine.

"Thank you, gentleman."

She moved her waist gently, said in my ear, "Do you really want to do it with a teenager?"

I smiled. We toasted.

One more piece to continue completing the new model of Grethel.

The incense burned. The glasses clicked and a column of black smoke and flames engulfed a U.S. Army Jeep. It was a tangle of guts, blood, burnt flesh, and fabric within the SUV's frame. Several soldiers of the occupying army had died. A rocket from the Iraqi Resistance Army or a mine in the middle of the road? Grethel swallowed half the wine and set the glass on the floor. I didn't care to know the answer.

She removed my shorts. She stuck her fingers in my glass.

"Where's the TV remote?" she said.

I reached for it. She raised the volume.

"If you want, use it with me."

And again she dipped her fingers in my wine. Grethel drew wet circles on my penis. I tried to touch her, put my fingers inside her. But she dodged my hands. She put her tongue on the tip of my penis. She looked at me. She smiled. She winked. I let her go ahead.

She gently forced me onto my back. She stood up, and I was between her legs. She pointed to the remote control. I gave it to her and she gently put one end of the remote control in her vagina. She moved it slowly. Again and again. And exchanged the remote for my penis when she settled on me.

At times I gripped her buttocks with my nails, squeezing her neck, and pinched her, soft, on the tip of her breasts, harder around the waist. Grethel wrapped my arms around both of her wrists, leaned on them, and I was left adrift.

The next thing I knew of Grethel she had let go of my

hands and stopped. The newscaster was about to read a press release about the Pope's death. I had turned on the TV quite late and we had not yet heard the day's headlines. Until that time we were only aware of John Paul II's seriously ill health.

I wanted to say something and she put her fingers on my lips. We sat on the couch.

I raised the volume a little. I had been following Karol's condition for days and at times I thought that he would get better. But no. Irreversible septic shock and heart and respiratory collapse. In May of '81, the Pope survived several shots, but this time the germs, heart, and lungs played a bad joke on him.

I watched Grethel and she watched the newscaster.

The voiceover was giving details of the Pope's death: – Karol Wojtyla was born in Wadowice, Poland, on May 18, 1920, residing in Vatican City, died at 21:37 on April 2, 2005, in his apartment in the Apostolic Palace of the Vatican.

The cathode ray tube fired images of the faithful crowd in Saint Peter's Square. Some prayed, some cried, most simply expected. The story ended with archival fragments of the Pope's visit to our country.

Grethel had crossed her arms. She wasn't watching the TV anymore. I wanted to do something, but I only managed to hold the TV remote. I couldn't say anything, because I saw her feet up on the sofa, because her arms were wrapped around her legs until she looked like a ball, and because she finally rested her chin on her knees. I tried to hold one of her hands.

"Just let me be, please," she said.

However, she didn't resist. I wanted to hug her, but this time she dodged and picked up her sweater.

She got up. She began to dress on her way to the bathroom.

I turned the volume down. I wanted to know how

they would choose a new pope and who the candidates were.

While Grethel was showering, I proposed that we sleep together that night. A soothing pill and several hours of sleep would help her recover. But she made a gesture of denial. Then I went to the bathroom. This time I could hold her, but in my arms there was nothing. She wiped her tears, took a long drink and said, "Sorry, I'm going home."

"Stay. Wasn't there something you wanted to talk about with me?"

"I'd better be going."

She slipped from my embrace. I barely resisted and went to the living room.

The newscaster began to read an official statement about the days of mourning. I got dressed and decided to settle down so that I wouldn't miss any detail. The Foreign Minister was speaking to the press.

Too much fuss.

And I called to Grethel.

"You must see this."

The Cardinal appeared on the news. They would say a homily.

"What do you think?" I said. "The Cardinal is on the news."

"I don't know what to believe."

From her backpack, she took out the box with the CDs.

"I'll come on Monday, we'll talk more calmly then."

I was about to curse the death of Karol, to throw the remote at the screen and have it explode into pieces at the Cardinal, the Minister of Foreign Affairs, and the newscaster. It seemed a conspiracy against me. I was exhausted. If I had decided to put aside my projects, it was to rest and be with Grethel. And she decided to leave without any explanation.

With the official note they repeated the footage of the

Pope's visit, during which he requested that Cuba become open to the world and that the world do the same with Cuba. Before me, John Paul II met with thousands of worshipers in the old Civic Square. From a huge print, hanging on the facade of the National Library, an immense Christ blessed the Square, all the devotees, hundreds of spectators, politicians, security agents, and the silhouette of the face of Che—bent steel beams reproducing with simple strokes that famous photo of the guerrilla commander taken by Korda—embedded in the front wall of the Ministry of the Interior building. All of this came in bursts from the cathode ray tube and I thought that they had hit the bullseye in my Grethel.

They shot and I was not unscathed.

"It's okay, go. Take your CDs."

I opened the door.

"I'll leave you these. I'll come back on Monday."

We said goodbye.

I closed the door.

I had plenty of food and alcohol for the weekend. I checked my phone book, found the number of a friend, but in the middle of the conversation I made up an excuse to hang up on her. I didn't have the energy.

I looked for the bottle of wine, the CDs, turned on the computer, and my audio equipment.

I started to drink the music collection bit by bit.

After Grethel left, I became aware of the phone. A long and stressful waiting in which I didn't want to dial her neighbor's number. A terrible wait. I could barely read half a page without returning to the beginning of the paragraph.

I could sit down and open my *Cuaderno de Altahabana* twenty days later. I was rereading the dates and notes when I got a call. It was Grethel's friend Patricia. I told her that I was alone and that I had gone more than two weeks without seeing her friend.

"Maybe Grethel is at home with her parents?"

"Ahmel, she didn't want you to know. She's been hospitalized."

I wrote down the room number and the hospital bed. They had discovered a tumor in one of her breasts. The pieces of my calendar were to change again.

She was lying in bed. Upon entering the room, I couldn't help but stare at her breasts. Grethel could neither talk nor look at me. At times, she contorted her face.

"It's the chemotherapy," Patricia said and stood up to greet me.

I felt ridiculous. I wanted to talk, but I was frozen. I was torn between saying hello to Grethel and saying something that could serve as consolation. Instead I just seemed to become more and more awkward. I took Grethel's hand, kissed her forehead. After greeting Patricia, I tripped over the rocking chair that she had been sitting on.

I looked at Grethel's face. And her arms: A purple bruise around the punctures. And her breasts: A single breast under the fabric of the sheet.

Grethel got up.

"Would you excuse me?" She said. "I need to go to the bathroom."

As soon as Grethel closed the bathroom door, I asked Patricia with a gesture to go out to the balcony.

"She has cancer and dysplasia," she said. "She was slow to come to the doctor."

"And after these drugs?"

She shrugged. "What can I say to you? I guess wait and see."

I returned to the room.

Grethel turned to me. I wanted to take her hand.

"Don't say anything. You know I'm afraid of words. Whatever you decide will be fine."

There was still fifteen minutes in the visit, but I said goodbye to Patricia, to Grethel.

And left.

During my second visit, Grethel asked me not to return. She preferred Patricia's company or to be alone. Her friend would keep me aware of her condition, send me a notice as soon she was discharged.

Soon, I got the call.

We agreed to meet at Grethel's apartment. It was difficult to choose a gift. I dismissed bringing a bouquet of flowers or a cake, and decided on some CDs instead: A selection of Brazilian music, Maria Callas, and Edith Piaf.

She was waiting for me, dressed in the same casual clothes she wore on her last visit to my house. She had covered her shaved head with a bandana. She smiled. I must have smiled too because she hugged me, it was strong, and I squeezed her.

"I told you once that I'm not at all modern. You see, I cry like a fool and all because of that damn music."

"It is lethal; now I know."

"Pure metastasis," she smiled. "I can't do anything but keep listening."

And I showed her my gift.

She read the credits. Each disc made her smile. I never imagined Grethel as a great music lover. She seemed to hear the music of each song, the lyrics, even just by reading the album covers she seemed to be with Callas and Piaf in the room of that house.

"You will end up killing me," she said.

And we laughed. And our hands touched. And we got close. Too close.

I had her face, her breath, the sound of her breathing at no distance at all from me. Breath. Perspiration. A faint scent of violets. The slightly salty taste of my sweat. Grethel pushed the door with her foot and then wrapped me in her hands.

We threw the CDs on the couch.

Her?: Straddling me. Me?: Against the wall.

Lips, neck, saliva, my sweat, scent of violets. Grethel was trying to take off my sweater. I also couldn't undress her with only one hand. So we got on the couch. Then I tried to take her sweater off —without wanting to, the scarf on her head got caught in the pullover and fell to the ground, exposing her whitest, bare scalp.

We looked at each other. She was tilting. She fixed her scarf and covered her chest with her arms.

She decided to get dressed. She picked up the sweater and stood in front of me. She wasn't hiding her bust.

I walked to where the CDs were. I picked them up. I knew in detail the credits of the covers, yet I couldn't understand what I was reading now.

"Do you want me to put one on?" I said.

"Maybe Piaf. *La vie en rose?*"

I looked at her. She apologized. I took her hands and left the CDs. We said goodbye.

With a few phone calls I managed to book a place in the computer lab. I had written down a message to Grethel on a piece of paper. It was just a short note that took me all night to write. I had to listen to her albums among coffee cups, deletions, and short walks from the desktop to the balcony, to make sense and finish it. Fitzgerald, Piazzolla, Bola, Miles Davis & Charlie Parker, Eric Clapton's blues. Holiday and Louis Armstrong at dawn.

Grethel : *albahaca_75@yahoo.com*

I left. Paid for a taxi. Amused myself with the fragments of a city that passed through the window. It was midmorning and there were only two occupied computers in the computer lab. A girl assisted me. It was not the same one as usual. She asked my name. I got to choose a computer.

The girl was tall, with curly auburn hair. A sweet voice. I couldn't avoid her eyes. Maybe it was her smile, the way of her lips, her eyes, but her face shared certain features with a cat.

I opened my bag, took out the paper with the message. I turned to the girl. She smiled. She was a rare beauty, a very beautiful woman.

As I opened my mail, I read the words several times. And decided not to send the message to Grethel.

I closed the program, got up, thought about going to the seawall; I was near the coast, the bay just a couple of blocks away.

"Are you done?"

"I'm going to sit a while at the seawall. Do you like the sea?"

"Yes, especially all of the fish. I would join you, but I can't close until six."

"How about if we go fishing? I am very good at cooking. I'll come for you?"

"Who will have to make the dishes?"

I looked into her eyes, she didn't look away, her eyes locked on mine.

"We could negotiate it."

I asked her name.

"Moonlight."

A rare and beautiful name. I said goodbye to the feline girl and went on my way to the sea.

A Burden, For What?

Story by Michel Encinosa Fú

Translated by Alison Macomber

Daniela killed herself. She burned her brain; this is what I'm referring to.

In the bathroom of the theatre, they said. When the power went out. She broke open an outlet, grabbed the cables, and peeled them back with nail clippers. Afterwards, she stabbed her skull with scissors twice, then put the cables through. Into her brain. They say that this doesn't hurt, and neither does a quick bite to the brain. Then she sat on the toilet, they said. And when they turned the electricity on again, the voltage and the amps came and went as they desired. You should've seen it, they said. You could see into her skull through the holes in her head, can you believe it? And her underwear was wet. And all of her makeup was still intact. Daniela wasn't one of those fairy faggots that cried, they said. But she's the one that pissed herself, they said.

None of them were there, but they keep talking about it. And I believe them. I thank them, and I walk down the sidewalk in the shade because the red-blue police carnival is already driving me crazy. It's a beautiful day. A little bit of sun, little clouds, an incredible transparency.

"Hey, they told me that a crazy chick killed herself in there." Gloria jumps toward me, with her eternal smell of trash. "Were you there? How was it? Hey, what the fuck are you laughing at?"

"It's a beautiful day," I said dodging her hand trying to grab my arm.

"That happened because someone wanted it to and he pressed a few buttons in his office."

It's true. It's horrible. It's like remembering that my

stomach is full because a calf was butchered a few days ago. No. It's worse than that. It's like being the butcher who dismembered the calf. Gloria insists: "How was it? Was it because she was having an affair? Or did they tell her she had AIDS? Tell me you faggot."

"It's not important to you," I said. "Stick your tongue up your ass."

She spits on my feet and heads toward the mountain of trash that spills over the buildings' trash bins. I stare for a few seconds while she begins to sniff, to rummage, to salvage. I'm tired of looking at it. Every day the same corners, the same trash bins. This is Gloria of the neighborhood. She who eats what you shit. She who wears anybody's clothes. She who collects cigarette butts at the bar. She who enjoys this city as a free supermarket. You know, Jesus, so young...

Broken spandex over her butt. Tan skin with no cellulite. Skinny and harsh body. Spiked and ashy hair. So young. I turn my back and continue toward Barcelona Street. I walk around the Capitol. I continue going down toward Brazil Street, until I catch a glimpse of the bay in the distance. I walk, contemplating my shadow which moves ahead of me, until there's no shadow to think about. At some moment, I don't know when, the whole sky was cloudy. I tend to be slow at noticing these kinds of things.

People always told me, "Don't go around breaking girls' hearts. And certainly not the hearts of young girls. The younger, the worse." Ten years ago, Daniela was seven years old and I was seventeen. Ten years ago, we were both hungry. Like siblings, we slept in the same bed in our poor building lot; it was her fault that I was late to discover nocturnal masturbation, serene and solitary. But I never reproached her. I never reproached her for anything. Not for her slaps or for her tantrums from her nightmares. Instead, I said to her:

"Imagine that, Dani, my dove. Can you imagine? Harley

Davidson. You know what a Harley Davidson is? A bike like the one uncle Patricio has. But bigger, like a sofa. And you and I on it, on the road, can you imagine? On a freeway like in the movies, you know, Kansas, Arizona, Omaha, Salt Lake City, sun, big sky, straight, always straight, into the cloudy horizon, into the horizon where lightning always falls, you know, can you imagine, my dove? You see the bolts cut the air, but the motor of the Harley won't let you hear the thunder, and then you go ahead and it never rains, because the clouds are running from us, and there is almost no grass, and everything is quiet, the Harley's motor, and you laughing, and I accelerating and accelerating, can you imagine?"

"Yes," she answered, "and we'll do that one day?"

"Just as I said it, my dove, one day, one day we'll do all of that."

Yuri sometimes came. He listened to us for a while and then left. Yuri was a very boring older brother because he was never hungry. He left the university to sell marijuana and PC components. Yuri was the one who pushed mom to send me to the weekday boarding school. "We're very cramped here," he said. "My clients come here, they see all of these people, and then they get nervous."

Afterwards, somehow Yuri found a husband for mom so she could leave too. "And don't you worry about me taking care of Dani. She'll be better fed and attended to with me than she was with you two."

Mom left under pressure. I can't blame her. I left feeling pressured. Daniela never forgave me. Seven years. Daniela was seven years old when I broke her heart, and she never sent it for repair. She started liking the bubbling of her broken teapot. Dandling it through the nights, she put a different rhythm in her life.

When I came to visit, I laid beside her, just like before, and I talked to her about the festivals at the Dunlop curve, during Mardi Gras, and in San Francisco. "Quit talking shit," she said to me, and turned to the other side. Yuri sometimes came, and he looked at us like we were pathetic.

Yuri is sitting at his desk, alone. The Sergeant is standing up, leaning on the wall, smoking. But he doesn't count. Yuri builds a domino wall. He knocks it down with his finger:

"I've already heard."

I sit in front of him, gather some dominos, and make them look like Stonehenge. These type of things always intrigued Daniela. Dolmens, menhirs, whatever. Neolithic drunkenness, all that shit.

"We have to move on. You heard me, Omaha. You have to get rid of the burden," he says, as he raises his head. "What do you got there?"

A man enters the room pushing a child ahead of him:

"You can stay with him tonight, but tomorrow I'll be here early to pick him up. Give me the usual."

"And what's the rush?" Yuri measures the boy with his eyes, and the boy smiles at him.

"He's my sister's nephew. So that's the hurry. The usual, I told you."

The man leaves. Yuri gets up and tells the child:

"Come here."

I follow them. In the back room, Yuri sits the boy on the bed, and puts a ham and cheese and TuKola soda in front of him, on a small table. For a while, Yuri watches how he eats and drinks, and then he gives him a Nintendo DS.

"I hate it when they bring them to me like this," he comments. "They don't even last for a night."

I shrug my shoulders and return to the living room. The Sergeant is in front of the table, roughly groping a domino. He blinks like a boy in trouble, drops the domino, and returns his three hundred pounds of muscle and fat to his spot.

I put any DVD into the player and throw myself on the

couch. It turns out to be Wesley Snipes, with glasses and a sword. Just what I need. It begins to rain outside.

That night, two weeks ago, at the San Rafael Boulevard, it was also raining. Hector. Hector was my friend and desk-mate in elementary school. I used to borrow his pen. He let me play with the little soldiers he brought to school–his mom entirely unaware. His hair was very blonde, almost white, dry, and bristly. Not much had changed.

"Omaha," Hector said to me, "make a decision, we're not going to stay here all night."

Daniela looked at me scared. So did the other girl, her friend. When he was a boy, Hector was a loner. He only played with me. Now his company had changed. And it had multiplied. A lot.

Those five guys seemed to be able to wait all night, but maybe they weren't going to. At least, they seemed impatient to me when they stopped us and brought us to the garage. I am not your rolling wheels, I am the highway... I am not your carpet ride, I am the sky... shouted Chris Cornell from the Panasonic on the hood of the Chevrolet. And he seemed to believe it.

"Your brother is crossing, Omaha," Hector said to me. "He's getting into my affairs. The fine flesh is his, okay, but the herb is my business. Because the pigs have sticks up their asses, the last thing I need now is competition. I have to send him a message, okay? It's not that I want to harm you, but I have to keep a good reputation with my partners, and with the neighborhood. That's it and nothing else, so relax, because nothing's going to happen to you, but, make up your mind. Which of the two?"

The two stopped looking at me.

"Do it. Your sister or your girlfriend?" You tell me.

"And all of this, I can just tell my brother that you, at knifepoint..."

"What knife? Do you see any knives here? A knife? Do you think we need that?"

I looked at them. Hector had grown a lot. Quite a lot. Also, the others had too. I vaguely remember them from elementary school. No. They didn't need anything like that.

Daniela's friend was still holding one of the sunflowers that the actors had given to the public. The play was entertaining. Many children in the audience. Much laughter.

"Take my sister away from here," I said at last to Hector. "I don't want her to see anything."

The guy shakes his umbrella out at the door, toward the outside, and enters.

"You have anything?" he asks.

Yuri nods. The man pulls out his wallet.

"And what about the other stuff?"

Yuri nods.

"Thank God." The man puts two bills in front of him, on the table. "Today I fought with the labor union, over those payrolls from last week I told you about... And I'm pissed off. And when I get back home my wife will surely want me to take her out to the movies, and my daughter is pissed at her husband, and every time she comes and starts talking shit and..."

Yuri continues to nod. While nodding, he takes some joints out of his pocket and gives them to him. The man goes to the back room.

"Give me one," I say to Yuri.

"No," he replies. "Not unless you pay for it."

"Well damn, I'm your brother."

"The worst thing in the world is debt between brothers."

Voices. The man's voice. I believe I also hear the child. I'm not sure.

They pulled Daniela out of my sight. Two of them grabbed the other girl. Hector turned up the volume. I didn't look at her face, while I unbuttoned her jeans. While I pulled down her jeans. While I pulled her underwear down.

She had a belly button piercing. A tiny Chinese lion's head, with a tiny gem. Maybe it was just a piece of glass. Yeah, that's more likely. I felt the tip of Hector's boot on my butt:

"Not like that. Do it from behind. So that she feels you. So that you both feel it, her, and you."

They turned her around. They pushed her forward onto the hood. I thought that the best thing to do was to end this as soon as possible, so I acted accordingly. She behaved herself well. She didn't scream.

"Okay," said Hector when I zipped my fly up. "Tell your brother to keep his fingers out of my business. And you were great, really. Just ask her."

I turned my face, very slowly. Daniela was behind me, in the doorway of the garage. She was trapped between the two, with a handkerchief stuffed in her mouth. They had her there the whole time. Her jeans below her knees. A third guy, behind her, stepped away from her.

Daniela let out a breath she seemed to have been holding for centuries. The guy zipped up his fly. I don't know which was worse. If she had seen me, or if I had seen her. Or to know that she had seen me, or to know that she knew that I knew that she had seen me, or to know that she knew that I had seen her. Maybe I should've asked the other one, her girlfriend, which was worse. But I never did. I never saw her again. Daniela didn't either, I think.

The woman leans against the doorframe; she's pissed-off.

"Hey, Yuri, and what about mine? Are you going to pay me or not? Look, I don't want to mess with you, but don't you know the meaning of respect?"

Yuri stretches in his chair.

"I have your money, girl. But it wouldn't be right for me to let go of it now. It's that I'm going to make a kind of investment, and it could start at any time... I have one for you back there. Head to the back and give me until Thursday. Look, so you see that I'm not cheating you..." He pulls out a wad of cash and fans it out. "Yours is here, but like I already told you... Of course, if it bothers you that much, I'll gladly, by all means..."

"You know how it is, Yuri..." she comes in and stands beside me. She smells divinely good. "But I don't think there's a problem until Thursday."

And she heads to the back room. Yuri puts the cash away, and lights a joint. He blows smoke in my face.

"Don't look at me like that. You've never known what business is all about."

And that's true, but it's because I'm Omaha, you know. Omaha, the guy with the happy face. The one who crosses the street without being touched by the sun. The one who doesn't get wet when it rains on the beach. The one who knows how to talk with children. The one who sells his only pair of shoes today and tomorrow he gets a free bike. The one who never pays, but always invites. The one who tries to walk to church, but comes back from the cabaret. The one who is on everyone's lips, and to everyone, he's honey. Or good, cold beer. Or melted cheese. Or a snapper fillet. Depending on what one prefers. The one who came to stay. The one who is always leaving. The same, yeah, Omaha. The one I wish you were, Omaha.

Outside it doesn't stop raining, but I have to go. It's that, or I'll go crazy.

The rain makes Gloria's smell at least bearable. She doesn't realize that I'm behind her, looking at her ass, until a few minutes pass of her being lost in excavation. She turns to me with arms full of empty bottles.

"Hey, gimme a hand, come on."

To her surprise, I say yes. We put the bottles in a sack that's already filled half way with I don't even want to know what kind of crap. We drag it one block, two blocks, in the rain, until she announces:

"Here it is."

I follow her into the darkness of the hallway. Stairs. Her, ahead. I miss a step and fall face down onto the sack. It was softer than I expected. We continue. Door, padlock, key.

"Go."

I manage to make out a bench and I sit on it. Gloria throws me something like a towel and tells me to take off my shirt. I obey. She turns on the light, and the first thing I see are her tits. Beautiful tits.

"You look like a wet cat," she says, pulling her t-shirt to the floor. "Come here. You must've come here for something."

She goes through another door and turns on another light. I follow her. The last room was a warehouse full of sacks and garbage bins. That didn't surprise me. This one did. Books stacked to the ceiling, lovingly compressed. In a corner, a kerosene stove. In another, a bare mattress. In another, some clothes on hangers. That's it. And Gloria naked. I didn't notice when she took off her spandex and her sneakers. I'm still slow, very slow.

"We have to hurry," she says. "My man will be here in a little bit."

And why not? Every woman has the right to have a man. Even the Glorias.

"And your man, what does he do? Does he also dumpster dive?"

"Not at all. He's in charge of a lot of money. He does business."

"Quit fucking around. What kind of business man would want to get mixed up with a dirty girl like you?"

"Hey, come on, yeah, that's my man, the owner of the neighborhood. His name is Hector. And don't tell me that you don't know him."

"Hector. The blonde, the herb man?"

"That's the same guy. You shouldn't be surprised. A ton of men like women like me, who know how to move. He ain't fucking with no one else. I am the one he likes. He always brings me presents."

71

I approach her. She opens her arms. I hit her twice, rapidly, in the face. She collapses onto the mattress, blood pouring from her nose.

"Son of a bitch, faggot, what the fuck is wrong with you?!"

"I don't like women like you."

"You're crazy, you faggot."

"If Hector asks you, tell him it was Yuri."

"And who is Yuri, you dick?"

"I am Yuri," I say to her, and I leave her there, bleeding.

I was the one who invited Daniela and her friend to go to the movies that night. Should I feel guilty about this? It was me who said, "We'll take the boulevard." Should I feel guilty?

Yuri's at the same door; he looks perturbed. I look inside. Four of them are playing dominos. Another two are smoking and looking out the window, without talking. The Sergeant is in the middle of the hallway that goes to the back room, and struggles with the Nintendo DS.

"I hate when this happens," Yuri said to me. "Too many people. But given that it's really raining... If I had at least two or three more... It's a good day to win big, and I'm out of stuff to offer... Any ideas?"

I shrug. What do I have to say? A man comes out of the back room, and passes by the Sergeant. Yuri nods to the other, who rushes to the back. The one that just came out comments to Yuri.

"You better give him a bath..."

And he leaves in a hurry.

"Omaha, do me a favor, put the heater in the bathroom," Yuri said to me. "And fill the bathtub. And get me a pair of clean sheets from the closet too."

I obey. The back of the closet in Yuri's room is the wall of the other room, the back room. I can overhear something. I can't hear much, but I still can hear it. Anyway, I didn't listen long. I'm sick of hearing it.

Dani went more than a week without talking, without crying, without going out to the street. Almost without eating, without sleeping. "I can't stand it, Omaha, I can't stand it, why didn't you do anything?"

I told her to go to the doctor, to get drunk, or sleep. She ignored me.

"Are you almost done?" Yuri pokes his head into the bathroom. "Two just got here, and one pays well."

"I'm almost done," I reply.

He fries me an egg, and he leaves. I reach my hand into the water. It's still warm. The boy looks at me for the first time. I hold his gaze. It's easy. Too easy.

"Get in here, sit down, lean forward so I can wash your back, get up, lift that foot, now lift the other, sit back down, turn around, close your eyes so the shampoo doesn't get in…"

It's too easy. And I like that. I dry him, I dress him, I push him out, I leave him in the back room, and I signal to Yuri. He, without wasting a second, calls to a man who could be our grandfather.

"He has a couple of bruises, and some scratches," I said to Yuri. "So I turned the light off and left nothing else on besides the lamp. You know some clients don't like that."

"You're learning," he says.

And it's true. I am learning. Finally. Not much, but something. Enough. At least, I hope so.

Today, when Daniela told me that she wanted to get ice cream, and then that she wanted to go to the movies, and then that she wanted to go to the theater to see her friends' rehearsal, I felt happy. Now I feel really stupid.

The Sergeant scornfully smacks the old man as he forces him out of the room, without hurting him too badly. We've all had a bad day. We've all had one bad day after another. We will have even worse days, until the days run out. Until we're all finished.

The old man leaves, crying. The boy, in the bed, up against the wall, shakes. Yuri brings some pills. I look at him wondering, and he explains:

"To pick-him-up."

I nod. To pick-him-up, whatever that means. Whatever it is. Amphetamines. Tonics. For high-performance athletes. For desperate ministers. Antidepressants. Hallucinogens. For housewives. For the Santería gurus of the online new wave. Analgesics. For everyone. Perhaps, all of that at the same time. Different kinds of pills. There are so many pills. Or simple placebos, maybe. That's the most likely.

"There's hot coffee in the kitchen," Yuri tells me. "Bring me a glass."

I go, pour him the equivalent of a cup, and return.

"I said a glass," Yuri raises his voice. "A complete glass. Filled to the brim."

I go, pour it, and return. Yuri forces the boy to roll over and sit on the edge of the bed, while the Sergeant splits the pills with his fingers and drops them into the coffee. Maybe they are not placebos, after all. They boy just looks at the floor.

"Go ahead, take it." Yuri puts the glass up to the boy's face.

After a struggle, and some splashes of coffee on the sheet, the glass is empty... No, but at the bottom there's still sediment. It's quite thick. Yuri gives the glass to the Sergeant, who goes to the kitchen and returns stirring another full glass.

"Go ahead, don't play the fool with me," Yuri begins the second round.

His small enemy surrenders without much of a fight. After emptying the glass, he coughs.

"A soda," Yuri orders.

I go. On the way I grab a beer for myself. I take long sips, while the boy hastily drinks the soda.

"Are there many left?" Yuri asked.

"Two," replied the Sergeant.

Yuri nods, and grabs the boy by his shoulders.

"Good, well, nothing happened. Be a man, and then I'll give you something."

The boy doesn't respond. Yuri takes his silence as an okay, and the three of us go, leaving the boy alone. Leaning out the window, I look at my hands. For the first time, I notice that my pinky is slightly separated from the rest, at the base, and begins a little lower than the rest. I wonder if everyone's hands in the whole world are like this. Or maybe it's just a deformation. Intrigued, I try to see Yuri's hands. I can't see them. He has them in his pockets. I try to look at the Sergeant's hands, but he always has them in fists. I try to remember Daniela's hands. It's useless. I only remember–I think–that they were weak.

How much force is necessary to penetrate a skull with scissors? How long do I have to wait?

"Forget about it," Yuri appeared next to me. "Forget about Dani. Have some balls, and forget about her."

I think I see sadness on his hardened face. I begin to regret it. Who knows, maybe it won't turn out well. The Sergeant is tough, and big, but I've never seen him work. I'm sure that he can deal with two, and maybe three, even four, but who knows. Hector is the owner of the neighborhood, and the neighborhood is full of a lot of people. And Yuri... Yuri is my brother. He's as skinny as me. That's why he has the Sergeant. My brother, the only one I have now. I should...

"She was a bitch anyway," Yuri says. "She was a whore, Dani. A good whore. It's better like this."

I stare at him.

"I started to fuck her after you left for Grandma's house. Dani liked it, from the beginning. She also loved when I would take pictures. I discussed this with my partners, and then I showed them the pictures. And then one asked me if he could be with Dani. I thought he was joking, but he was serious. He told me he'd give me money so our friendship would remain cool. I said yes. And then to my other partners. Dani liked it, not as much, but she continued liking it. Then a woman brought me a girl. She was her husband's daughter, not her own, and she left her with me every Wednesday, when her husband was on duty. She said fifty-fifty. That seemed okay to me... And so we progressed. When Dani got a little older, she told me one day that she didn't want to keep doing it. I told her that was fine; that she was no longer needed. She told me to never tell you. I also said that was okay. But now that doesn't matter... Can you imagine? She loved that I called her 'my dove,' like you used to say...

"And it seems impossible, after all of the wood hammered through all of her holes, that she cracked only because they did it to her, then... Yeah, I found out about that, although neither one of you told me anything. Also they told me you were very good... But that doesn't matter. Want me to show you pictures of Dani, when she was a little girl? I still have them on hand."

I don't see anything on Yuri's face anymore. It's just a simple, hardened face. Nothing more than that.

"Seriously, you don't want to see them?" he insists. "You can even have them. Really. My gift to you. And if you don't want them, they're the Sergeant's gift."

I tell him no. I say I don't need them. He can do whatever he wants with them. I look at the street, then the corner, and I tell him that I have to go to the bathroom.

As we watched the rehearsal, I noticed that Dani had

been silent for a while, absorbed in thought. I thought I knew what was bothering her, and I hugged her shoulders.

"All you have to do is tell yourself that nothing happened. And if you say it enough, it's true. Because it's true. Nothing happened. To me, you're still Daniela, my dove. And if you want, when you're feeling better, I can tell Yuri, and you'll see how the Sergeant, Yuri's shadow, will give Hector and all of the others a suppository of The Morro Lighthouse..."

It occurred to me that it was a witty and convincing speech, and, proud of myself, I smiled at her while she told me, smiling, to wait a minute, while she went to the bathroom. I kept smiling when the lights went out. I even smiled when the lights came back on, when somebody screamed in the bathroom, when everyone began running all over the place. How dumb.

From the bathroom window I lost sight of Hector and his guys, his "animals," who, by now, should be at the door. There are like six or seven of them. I'm not so sure about what's going to happen. I'm not even sure what I want to happen.

Voices. Shouting. Gloria's name. Shouting. Daniela's name. More shouting. A bang on the table. Another slam. More yelling. The volume lowers. It keeps going. Voices. Isolated words. Silence.

I leave and head toward the living room. Yuri and Hector sitting at the table. On the table, some bills. A bottle of rum. Glasses. Serious faces, quiet. Men at the table. Affairs of men.

"When I find the one who broke my bitch's face, I'll break his balls," Hector says, and he seems to repeat it four or five times. "No one lays a hand on one of my women like that... And much less, no one tries to involve a business partner of mine like that..." He lifts his gaze toward Yuri. "In fact, it's not your fault that your sister was such a pussy and an asshole."

Yuri nods:

"Family isn't upon request. That would be nice... But anyway, about our deal, let's meet tomorrow at the bar, and discuss it thoroughly, with clear heads. You'll see that we really do agree."

"Yeah, hell, I'm sure of it."

"Omaha," Yuri cocks his head in my direction, "go to the corner and buy a couple of bottles. I have some soaking wet friends here and their bodies need to be warmed up. Take those with you." He points to the bills on the table.

The Sergeant and the animals group around the pictures he holds. They laugh. They click their tongues. In one of the pictures I glimpse Daniela's smile. A dumb blonde's smile, like Britney Spears', the kind of smile that Daniela knew always made me laugh.

"The good kind or the cheap kind?" I ask Yuri, and I grab the bills.

"The good kind, hell, everything is going well."

From the back room comes the voice of a man and a crying child. Yuri, Hector, the Sergeant, and the animals, laugh. And I also smile, and go out into the street in the rain, to get the bottles, laughing, because, really, as usually happens when there are men who know what they're doing, everything is going well.

Summer Bells

Story by Jhortensia Espineta Osuna

Translated by Alison Macomber

Dunia, your daughter, doesn't leave her room, or the room that you both share and that you all shared with your mom and your grandmother until they decided to die last June, one after the other, so August wouldn't remove the liquid that remained between their skin and bones.

Through the window, the neighborhood parades by, wearing their Sunday clothes. Others only pass with their nylon bags to begin the week with whatever is in the bag.

It's the end of the month; you're trapped between the window and the cracks on the floor where the ants have made small colonies. The living room is large, with only corroded furniture incapable of filling the territory. The painted wall exhibits your title "Doctor of Medicine," along with your white coat and your stethoscope. The three things hang on the thickness of the adobe wall of lime and cement.

You don't move from where you stand and you look at the old man with the dog on the front sidewalk. Since his son arrived, the old man is in better condition. His ribs are no longer visible underneath his skin, and maybe he doesn't need to kill cockroaches at night, filling the floor with insects and gobs of spit.

You still haven't moved from this spot; you continue standing there between the cracks on the floor. The old man pets the dog's belly as he lifts his leg and urinates on the wall.

"Bringing that dog here cost two thousand dollars!"

Your whisper surprises you and you look out the window.

The old man enters behind the dog, and then he closes the door behind him.

"A dog!"

The old man's son arrived in a car one night, filling the block with noise and music. When he left, he was just a boy lacking many aspirations other than seeing his father killing cockroaches and spitting everywhere. Now he is a mixture of grease and odors; with him he brought a fat woman as greasy and odorous as he and they filled the house with furniture capable of holding him, his fat woman, and an entire family of smelly, obese white people.

The first time the fat man saw Dunia he offered her a soda. They spoke intensely about her slenderness and her blue eyes, but mostly about her slenderness and how much she had grown. He called the fat woman so that Dunia could meet her; to know about her obesity and the little Spanish she spoke. But you didn't pay attention to that; in the end you were just old neighbors.

One night they went out. Dunia returned a little dizzy. You had never seen her so playful or perhaps you had never paid attention to her stature, nor to her breasts. It wasn't simply her fifteen years; but that they were thin, long, and well-developed years, even if the ration basket was limiting her genetics.

But it was too much: Your mother, your grandmother, Dunia, and your plans to find a job abroad, even if there are or are not black people like there are here. By working abroad, you would be able to repair the floor, full of cracks, and fill the spacious living room with furniture.

The second time, the fat woman almost carried Dunia to the house. You smiled at her at the door. She carried a shopping-bag cluttered with stuff —so many things that the next day you could only caution her about the side effects of drinking.

"It was only two beers, mom."

And dancing. You knew later how much they had danced. "They are so much fun."

"It is the money that makes smiles," you said between grimaces, not only because of her alcoholic intoxication, but because of the fat couple's caring and tennis shoes and jeans and perfumes.

"Thank goodness they didn't forget the favors I did for their old man."

The following days everything was the same; your daughter barely came through the house to bring you food and give you a kiss. The fat couple smiled at you from the car, waiting for Dunia to get in to go any place in the city that would permit two, insatiable fat people and a teenager.

"They're leaving tomorrow."

Dunia almost jumped from the door of the house to the car, while August evaporated the city.

They brought her back in the small hours of the morning. This time she wasn't stumbling, but she wore an idiotic grin and her eyes were almost motionless. She went to her room and threw herself onto the bed. They gave you an even bigger smile, with an even bigger briefcase.

"She's a good girl, take care," said the fat woman in her ridiculous Spanish, and the fat man nodded his head.

As soon as they left, you opened the briefcase; you were examining all of its contents. Maybe they would take those clothes into account the next time they select someone for a job abroad. Those clothes and those perfumes relieved the burden of carrying two old women for years, and returned your tall daughter with the blue eyes to you.

When you counted the money Dunia approached with her hands on her face.

"My head hurts really badly."

"Your entire body must hurt."

"My head more than anything."

"Lie down, and it will pass."

Almost from the beginning, you knew it wasn't just beer. Her clothes carried a dry and thunderous odor of marijuana. You smelled her mouth many times while she was sleeping, and you sat on the bed and looked at her.

You felt an intense cold in your stomach, not from the smell of marijuana, not even from the remains of dried semen caught in her pubic hair, but because you remained unchanged and even felt pity for Dunia that she bore a weight so heavy or, perhaps, that your daughter was capable of maneuvering on top of the fat man.

Now you're at the window; you don't have to go to the market to haggle or wait almost until the end for the rebates. Sunday is all yours. Tomorrow you will go to work with much more eagerness to elude your patients' clinical, delirious diagnoses, more because of scarcity than their pathology, and to actually prescribe them the dose of humor that they need.

Dunia, from behind, surprises you by striking the bars one by one with the fan; you look at her and she smiles at you.

"They left you a suit that's beyond imagination."

"I already saw it."

"Come here so you can try it on."

The two crouch down to rummage through the briefcase.

"What would have happened if she surprised you with him?"

Dunia looks at you and wipes away the sweat on your brow.

"I never slept with him."

"Then who?"

"It was with her."

You keep looking and begin to rummage around in search of the suit.

"The semen that you cleaned off of me was from the dog."

The suit is the color purple; the blouse has a print in the same color and in black, with matching shoes. It is a nice suit, only it has to be taken in.

Four Cuban Writers Go To Paradise

Story by Carlos Esquivel

Translated by Karen González

Nicolasa Guillén, Virgilia Piñera, Regina Pedroso, and Josefa Lezama Lima leave to go to paradise for a week. However, upon arrival they find out that, in fact, they have arrived at the steps of a ramshackle hotel for writers where they must imagine that they've arrived at paradise.

In addition, they are forced to pay an astounding amount to stay there, and among the guests sharing paradise with them, there were infamous writers from many countries whom they always intuited to be literary disgraces.

Astonished, they looked at each other. Of course they couldn't quit. A week would go by quickly in paradise, said Nicolasa, who held the sign of "I am in charge here, and it will be done as I consider prudent."

Nicolasa Guillén, Virgilia Piñera, Regina Pedroso, and Josefa Lezama Lima stayed in ramshackle rooms, and that night, after a derisory dinner, they received an invitation to a literary gala where they would have to gulp down lectures delivered by several of those other, infamous writers.

Virgilia Piñera said that she would rather have a drink at a nearby bar. Nicolasa couldn't prevent it, for she too wanted to escape, but couldn't on account of her simulated officiality. The others, who wanted to demonstrate their fidelity to her under any circumstance, also stayed.

And so they slept pleasantly while their colleagues read somniferous poems.

Pleasantly? No.

While the reading took place, Nicolasa dreamed that in one of the streets of paradise she found a man who ate books by Cuban authors. They taste horrible, the old man said while chewing on a recently published novel. The worst ones are those by Nicolas Guillén, too coarse, as if the most artificial condiment was the author's very name.

When Nicolasa tried to reprehend the book eater, twist his neck, she woke up with her hands wrapped around the neck of a Costa Rican poet.

Regina Pedroso dreamed that she had committed suicide six times. Without success, or successfully, depending on your point of view. They were eccentric suicides. One of them consisted of living as a regular citizen in her own country. A voice inside the dream rumored that this oneiric episode was too exhausting, that no punishment could prove to be so drastic as that one.

She woke up startled, believing she was in her house, living and dying the suicide as the final punishment of her days. Then, relief ran through her for a few seconds.

Josefa Lezama Lima suffered from horrifying nightmares, night after night. As a result she was wary of those almost incomprehensible limits between dreams and reality. However, her wit had allowed her to create an intermediate point. She would jump from one place to the next with impenitent autonomy. What she could not control was the matter referring to the jump—to the moment of the jump. A moment that could last half a minute or a few hours. In that moment she did not belong to any of the two places. She tried to use her wit to find a way to penetrate those networks but it was impossible. During the jump she wasn't herself, she didn't belong anywhere, she didn't exist.

She later understood that she was both witness and part of one of those very suggestive metaphors in which death surrounds dreams, and she understood that Freud, Borges, or any other, would tremendously envy those sensations that governed her. Then, it would be necessary to understand that Josefa was neither asleep nor awake throughout the literary evening. She was in a place called "jump."

Upon seeing her friends asleep, Virgilia, arriving late,

decided, after sitting in one of the last chairs in the theater, to throw herself into the world of dreams like a docile damsel submerging into a docile and fantastic novel.

She didn't have any relevant dreams. She dreamed, instead, of flowers. Spectral and asleep, flowers.

Four Cuban writers went to paradise, but paradise was too similar to what they did not believe was paradise.

Judith

Story by Abel Fernández-Larrea

Translated by Alison Macomber

aunt elshvieta was about eighty years old. she was never married. she was small, with short hair and glasses, and her large nose protruded from under them. at first glance she didn't seem to have a gender. my father always said that she "looked like woody allen, the american film director." my mother always scolded my father every time that he, before an imminent visit from our aunt, dropped that comment. but our aunt, on the other hand, didn't come to visit us very often.

she and my grandmother were sisters, but for some reason they didn't speak. when grandma died, my father convinced our aunt to come and live with us at haifa. at first, she resisted, but ended up making the trip from biro-bidzhan to settle in our apartment. she lived with us for a month. at the end, our aunt said that she preferred to live alone and was thinking about moving back to trans-siberia. then my father told her that there was no need to return to any place and he rented an apartment for her close to ours in neve sha'anan.

she sometimes came over for rosh hashanah and other holidays, although none of us followed the tradition. however, she never missed yom hashoah, the day in which we remembered the holocaust. that day, while the majority of the neighborhood walked down the street or went to the synagogue, we made a simple dinner in which my mother prepared little pastries "like in khabarovsk." our aunt loved these pastries. she could eat ten in one sitting, and then she would say that she felt bad and that she should return to her house. my father always convinced her to stay, and he sent my brother and i to prepare one of the beds in our room for her. at night, my little brother slept with our parents, and i remained in the room with my aunt, which always made me a little apprehensive.

my aunt talked in her sleep. most of the time she said russian slogans, as if she was haranguing workers in a rally. my father told me that she had been commissar, working actively after the war. also, he told me that because of her, many had been expelled from the party, which was the equivalent of losing it all. people even went to the gulags because of my aunt. meanwhile, she had been awarded the order of lenin.

other times, when she slept, she spoke in yiddish. these dreams seemed older, from before or during the war. they were convulsive dreams. i didn't understand yiddish very well; only a few words. from what i understood, she seemed to talk with someone, saying "my love, my love, don't do it." sometimes she said the name of my grandmother. other times, she repeated a name: rudolf. several years passed before i could find the story, before i understood the cause of aunt elshvieta's dreams.

i was about to finish high school. i had read something about the great war, about the massacres, the evacuations, the death camps. i was interested in everything related to the german-romanian invasion and the resistance of the partisans. i thought that maybe aunt elshvieta, who had lived during that time, would know more about it.

one day, after i left school, i decided to stop by her apartment on my way home. my aunt wasn't there, so i had to sit on the steps and wait for her. after a while she appeared, laden with shopping bags. she was happy to see me and i thought that was a good sign, so i helped her carry the bags. my aunt, given her age, climbed the stairs more energetically than i did. i assumed this was because her habit of walking from one place to another when she was a commissar. we put the bags on the table. my aunt wouldn't stop looking at me and made comments about how much i had grown, even though it had only been a month since she'd been to our house.

"but how big you are, misha!" she said, "every time i see you, you look more like your father!"

then she offered me a snack and began to prepare orange juice. i walked over to her while she cut the oranges. she had a steady hand. with one chop she'd part the fruit into halves.

"aunt," i said, finally daring to speak, "can you tell me about the great war?"

her countenance changed. the knife stopped, skimming the surface of the orange. my aunt shook her head and continued driving the blade into the fruit. then she put the knife down and began to squeeze an orange half in her hand. her pulse was shaking.

"what do you know?" i said at last.

"i don't know... anything."

"our region was very far from the front. there is little i could tell you."

she finished squeezing the oranges. she added water and a little sugar and served me a glass with a cookie. i wasn't going to ask her again. i drank the glass in silence, nibbling the cookie between sips. after a while she had forgotten the incident and she repeated over and over that she was delighted by my visit. when i was leaving, she insisted that i bring some oranges to my mother.

for a month i frequently went to my aunt's house. i didn't ask her questions, but i knew that she was hiding something behind her reluctance toward this topic, and i harbored a secret hope that she would at some point decide to tell me. she, on the contrary, distracted me by inviting me to have snacks, sometimes tea and donuts, and other times juice and cookies. occasionally she would tell stories, but these were always about life in the autonomous region of trans-siberia. at first, they didn't arouse my interest. then i became accustomed to her stories of workers building their lives in adverse conditions.

one day i forgot to visit her. nothing special, only i had started to think about my exams and i gradually turned my attention to other issues.

that year aunt elshvieta was not with us on yom hashoah. she called by phone to tell us that she was indisposed, and that she was very sorry. my mother told her that she would save some khabarovsk cakes for her. even that didn't seem to cheer her up. after dinner, i went to my room to do homework and i was surprised to be missing my aunt, even if she did talk in her sleep in the middle of the night.

a week later, my father had to bring aunt elshvieta to the hospital. there they did tests and diagnosed her with a severe heart condition. they placed her in long-term care and they discussed the need to operate. mom and dad took turns staying with her. i was so busy with my exams that i was only able to visit her once. when i did, she was sleeping. i stayed a while, watching her dream, in case she woke up. she didn't wake up. nor did she say a word.

summer came along with the end of high school. i was concerned about college, and leaving home. my aunt didn't get better, but she expressed her reluctance toward any operation. at the beginning of elul they decided to send her home, to see if a more familiar environment would settle her. we put her in my room, in my brother's bed, and we brought some clothes and a box from her house that she insisted upon having.

once she arrived at our house i felt she didn't take her eyes off me. i was a little guilty about not visiting her frequently, and because i hadn't seen her that much while she was in the hospital. that night, while she was sleeping, she

spoke in yiddish the entire time. again and again she repeated the same words, the same names: that of my grandmother and the so-called rudolf. when i woke in the morning she had already gotten up. she seemed to have been
watching me sleep for hours.

"misha," she said to me when i opened my eyes, "come
here, come with me."

i stretched with a big yawn. i jumped out of bed and
sat on the edge of hers.

"i am going to tell you something that nobody knows.
something that i have kept quiet for a very long time."

i got the creeps. finally I would know the history of the
guerrillas fighting against the nazis.

"you see that box, the one they brought from my apartment?" my aunt pointed at it without taking her eyes off
me. "bring it to me, please."

it was a medium-sized box, lined with leather. the
hinges creaked when i took it, and when i dropped it on
the bed, the lid jumped up. inside were piles of paper,
cards, and medals. the lenin award was there, which cost
so many expulsion from the party. also, there were many
photographs. aunt elshvieta appeared in all of them,
dressed in a grey uniform and military boots. in some she
was walking through the trans-siberian snow, in others
she was in elegant offices, shaking hands with party lead-
ers, or being awarded for her political work. in all of them
she could be easily recognized: her short hair, her lack of
makeup, the hard look behind her glasses. however, one
photograph looked nothing like her. i only recognized her
through a familiar appearance, and because the photograph looked like pictures i had seen of my grandmother.
it was dated 1941, when aunt elshvieta was around twenty years old.

"ah, sweet youth," she sighed at the sight of the picture, "here i was before the war. i was eighteen."

in the other photograph, she appeared with my grand-mother, but wore a severe look and had short hair.

"this was around the days we came to birobidzhan," she said, "it was a such long trip on the train, very long."

her words gave me doubts. until then, i had thought that they, my grandmother and my aunt, had always lived in birobidzhan. i kept looking through the papers. suddenly, i couldn't believe it, in the bottom of the box was an einsatgruppen d stamp, the kind originally put on the collar of a jacket. i recognized it instantly because i had seen it so many times in history books. the stamp had an almost black mark on it that seemed like it was part of the fabric.

"oh rudolf, rudolf!" my aunt sighed, her eyes turning glassy.

i put the stamp back in the bottom of the box and lowered the lid. aunt elshvieta bowed her head and covered her face with her hands.

"in 1941," she began saying, "your grandmother and i lived in the village of bilivka, near vinnytsia, in ukraine. we were both diligent students of the regional school, and we were preparing to go to college. but the blitzkrieg came. the men had to go to war; only the very old and children were left. us women were left in the village to do all of the work. we cut firewood, carried the water, and fed the animals."

"one morning we heard gunshots near the village. the war was advancing toward us. we were all very afraid, so we hid in the basement of the rabbi's house. we were there, huddled, for two hours, thinking that at any moment the soldiers would arrive. then it was all over. there was a long silence, we didn't know what had happened, and fear prevented us from going and finding out. in the afternoon it was very hot so i decided to go to look for a bucket of water. there was very little water in the well, so i went to the river, carrying two buckets instead of one."

"i was coming back from the river when i saw him, lying

motionless under a fir tree. he was a young german soldier, and his leg was wounded. when i approached him he began to tremble. he said things that made no sense. i hesitated a couple moments, thinking about whether i should continue on and leave him lying there or if i should stop to help him. i finally decided to give him a little bit of water, cleaned the wound on his leg, and bandaged it using my handkerchief.

"i secretly went to see him every day for a week. i brought him food and water that i stole from the pantry, and cared for his wound as we conversed. his name was rudolf and he was lieutenant of einsatzgruppe d, but at that time i didn't know what that meant. he said he was against the war, that he did not want to kill anyone and that he only did so out of obligation. he said that in the year 39 he had begun to study literature, but then they sent him to the army and he had to leave the university. he would recite shiller's, hölderlin's, and novalis' poems, and when doing so his blue eyes would shine intensely."

"one day he wasn't there. with my care, his wound had healed and he could already walk. it saddened me that he left without saying goodbye, but i thought that it was better for him to return to his companions as soon as he could. however, the days passed and i found myself thinking about him most of the time."

aunt elshvieta approached the box. she opened it and began to review the photographs. she ran her hands over each one and then set them aside. she stopped when she came to the picture of her and my grandmother. she spent some time looking at it in silence. then she turned and looked for the stamp at the bottom of the box.

"some days later we heard the shots approaching us again. this time we heard very intense sounds like heavy artillery and tanks pushing through the forest. we went back to the basement to hide, and there we heard sounds of tanks coming closer. then we heard them stop, already in the village, and then the sound of boots and orders given in german. they were looking for us. the women sobbed, trying to prevent their children's crying. the rabbi led the old in prayer. your grandmother and i were clutching each other in a corner. not even the worst could separate us."

"it wasn't long before a soldier discovered our hiding place. they pulled us out violently, shouting insults in german, and took us to the center of the village. a boy tried to escape and one of the soldiers fired. a flash. the boy fell forward, dead, and his mother began to scream and hit the soldier, as he held her off with a rifle. another soldier grabbed the woman and pushed her to her knees. then an officer drew his gun and put it to the woman's neck. only a single shot. the woman fell headlong into the dust. i recognized the officer when he raised his head to put away the gun: it was rudolf."

"they told us that the next day they would take us to vinnytsia. from there, a freight train would take us to another place, where we would work for the reich. we would sleep there that night, and would leave very early the next morning. then they took us to a barn and locked us up inside."

"during the night some soldiers entered. they were drunk and laughing. they took the young women, telling us that there was a party. before leaving, a soldier asked if anyone had a musical instrument. matvéi, an old man, said that he had a violin. they also brought him with us."

"the barracks had been mounted in the rabbi's house, which was the largest one in the village. in fact, they had the party there. the house was full of drunk soldiers who began to whistle at us when we arrived. they told matvéi to play. he took out his violin and began playing a polka. the soldiers took us out to dance. they offered us cigarettes and cognac. i was looking at all of their faces for rudolf's blue eyes. i didn't see him."

"rudolf appeared quite later that night. many of the soldiers were lying in the corners, sleeping off their drunkenness. others had gone, leaving with the last girl they danced with. some of them tried to separate me and your grandmother. one soldier insisted upon leaving with your grandmother, but i wouldn't let her go. the soldier laughed with the others. 'what am i to do,' he said, 'it seems that i can have two fish at the same time.' the others laughed. they told him to share them. they tried to peel me from my sister, but we were seized by force and they were drunk."

"then rudolf entered. he asked what had happened and the soldiers explained it to him. he ordered them to leave me in peace. i thought that we would be saved, in spite of everything, because of rudolf. he came up to me and looked at me with that gleam in his eyes. i let go of my sister. 'and what do we do with the other?' asked one of the soldiers. he was referring to your grandmother. 'you can take her,' said rudolf. i screamed. i didn't want them to take your grandmother. i tried to grab her again, but rudolf stopped me, holding me back forcefully. the soldiers took her and i remained there, crying."

aunt elshvieta covered her face with her hands. i realized that she was reliving events that she had long kept hidden. i had never before heard anything about what had happened there. not even from my grandmother.

my aunt cried, squeezing the stamp in the palm of her hand. then she told me how rudolf had tried to take off her clothes, and that when she refused, he became enraged and began to hit her, yelling that she was a jew and that her entire race was going to die; that hundreds had already been killed in vinnytsia; that he, with his own hands, had shot more than twenty. then he took my aunt by force and brought her to the rabbi's room, where he continued hitting her and harassing her, before he tore her dress, overpowered her, and raped her.

"when he was done, i cried uncontrollably. i was badly beaten; my nose bled. My entire body hurt and i loathed myself and was very afraid. he lit a cigarette and smoked it on the edge of the bed in silence. when he was done, he threw the butt on the ground and crushed it with his boot, then he fell upon the pillow and fell asleep. i didn't want to move for fear of waking him, but i had to get out of there. i had to flee. at one point i mustered enough force and courage and got up very slowly. he didn't wake up."

"outside only drunk soldiers were sleeping. no one moved. i went out into the night, half-naked and bleeding. in the middle of the darkness i tripped over a pile of firewood. i feared that that the noise would wake the soldiers, so i groped and searched for an ax to defend myself. no one woke up, but a few steps away i heard a whimper. it was my sister; i recognized her voice even though she whispered. i approached her. she also was beaten and her dress was torn. she had been assaulted by several soldiers. her mouth was broken and her black eyes wept with fury, but they were without strength. an infinite rage came over me. i tightly grabbed the ax."

"in the room, rudolf was still asleep with his head cocked on top of the pillow. in that moment rudolf looked like he did under the fir tree, that injured boy who recited poetry. but nothing could erase the newer images of rape, humiliation, and beatings; the ease and coolness with which he had shot the woman; how he said that all of us jews were going to die; that he had killed at least twenty. i clutched the ax in the air and let it fall like a broadsword."

aunt elshvieta imitated the movement of the ax in the air. then she stood for a moment, with her head down, staring at her hands. in them was the stamp of einsatzgruppe d, with the mark almost as black as dried blood.

i imagined my aunt as a judith, a heroine who saved her village from invaders, decapitating their general. i imagined her brandishing the blonde-headed german lieutenant. bringing his head to her friends locked in the barn and freeing them. my aunt remained silent, bowing her head with her eyes fixed on the stamp.

"and what happened next?" i said without being able to resist the temptation of knowing if what i imagined was true: my heroine aunt freeing her village.

"then i went to look for your grandmother," she said, "i helped her to her feet and we slipped into the forest. we walked several days until we found our troops. we were put on a military train bound for birobidzhan and khabarovsk."

i looked at my aunt, surprised. that wasn't what i expected.

"but, and the others?" i said without understanding anything. "and old matvéi? and the other girls? and the others locked in the barn?"

aunt elshvieta sighed. she put the seal away into the box.

"the others? we never knew," said my aunt as she closed the lid, "imagine, if i would have freed them, we would have all been discovered! there were too many people."

Alone

Story by Raúl Flores

Originally written in English

She had the overwhelming feeling that we were alone in this world.

She said to me "Come and look thru the windows," and I went and looked around and could only be aware of the typical landscape of one of those ordinary evenights rounding October: Foggy shrubs smoothing sadly along deserted streets in the city, and the moon like a white giant patch across the darkened sky.

"Don't you realize?" she screamed, "Can't you see?" again she screamed and her voice multiplied echoes in the fall (can't you see? can't you see? can't you see?). "We're all alone", she whispered, "Totally alone in this world."

"What?" said I, "Why do you think so?"

"Don't you realize?" she screamed again, and her shouting was shooting in the middle of the night: Solitude standing, a stone cast towards the moon. She said "Let's go out. Somewhere. To see what's new."

I said yes. So she'd be quiet. I'd have given anything so she'd be quiet. To get all those crazy ideas out of her head. Her poor alienated little head filled with golden hair. Like a Barbie doll. And that's how I used to think about her sometimes: My little Barbie doll, lost in her little beautiful Barbie world, filled with broken dreams and lost illusions.

So I said to myself: Ok, Barbie, let's go out, let's be swallowed like Jonah by the fog of these restless times of October, let's be lovingly mugged by zealous maladroits in the midnight hour.

And so we did go out. The fog shrouded us in and we

walked and walked streets and streets and streets and miles and meters and square feet.

"See?" she kept saying, almost to herself. I could overhear her. And I could also see. Or (let's rephrase) I could not see. Not a soul. No one around. Miles and miles and not one anywhere. And so we walked, crisscrossing the city, perimeter, area, and diameter, and never we glimpsed anybody.

"See?" she said. "We're all alone." I was amazed. Alone in this world with my little beautiful Barbie doll of blonde hair and small ambitions. Alone. No music. No friends. No Saturday night matinee, no Sunday morning drives. Alone. No nothing. Like in a crystal bell. Like in a 3D cube. No lights, no colors whatsoever. Fog shrouding in, decuplicating time and time again. And there we were. All alone.

"Cannot be like this," I said to Barbie.

We went to a restaurant. We went to the movies. We went to a shopping mall, to the market, we entered empty churches. But there never was anyone around. I kept saying all the time "cannot be like this," but it was very likely that it could be like this, and it was.

She was silent. Had the look of a public funeral and glass in her eyes. Her small beautiful world had been smashed to bits and pieces.

"You have to understand," I said to her, but she was beyond comprehension.

"I don't get it," she whispered, "One day it's ALL here, and next thing you know, ALL'S gone. I don't get it," time and time again, "I don't get it," she said.

She stopped being a Barbie doll and became a wind-up toy. Well, I thought, we can do whatever we choose to do. Stay late in the cathedral. Start drinking and never stop, without ever having to worry about going to work on the next day. Free beers every day. Free food.

We could scream our lungs out and the cops would never come to check us out. Because there were no cops. There was no one, there was nothing. No people, no cats, no dogs. Nothing at all. Just clouds and wind and moon and fog. Nothing else. Her and me. No one else.

"Let's check some houses," I said to her. "Maybe some-one's home," I whispered.

We started entering people's houses. We started invading private places, spying alien motions. Frozen instants of lifetime perpetuity. Lovely living rooms decorated with bath curtains and Klee's paintings on the walls, dining rooms with giant sand clocks stopped in the ultimate grain of time, corridors filled with expensive books, cheap plastic toys scattered on the floor, black tiling, white tiling, tidy bathrooms, blood-stains over basement floors and, in some way, we knew that it had nothing to do with the things we were looking for.

LP's over kitchen shelves, pots and cans: A small universe for a small crowd of passers-by. House by house. Two, three, four. Six, seven, fifteen. And only in the 23rd house did we find a boy and a girl lying asleep over a bare mattress.

"Well," said my Barbie doll as her eyes faded behind tears. "We're not alone," she said and her voice broke.

They slept with a natural grace, inspiration, aspiration, just like an afterparty of strippers and sodden popcorn.

"I'm gonna wake 'em up," she whispered.

"Don't do it," said I, "they must be tired, let 'em sleep."

"I don't care," she said, "I'm gonna wake 'em up, they have to know what's going on."

And so she went and woke them up. I tried to stop her, but it was already too late. The sleeping girl had opened her eyes and winked in confusion.

"What's up?" the girl asked and I felt a knot in my throat at that very moment.

I just didn't know what to say.

Breaking News

Story by Jorge Enrique Lage

Translated by Guillermo Parra

*She doesn't mean a thing to me, and yet
I'll pursue the mystery of her death.*

—Rodolfo Walsh

They say the freeway will crisscross the city. What's left of the city. By day the bulldozers advance, sweeping away parks, buildings, shopping centers. By night I wander close to the sea, amid the ruins, the machinery, the containers, trying to catch a glimpse of the magnitude of what's coming. There is no doubt the freeway will be something monstrous.

This is what happens with freeways: It doesn't matter where they might pass through, on each side the desert begins to grow (like an intention of space, a possibility).

I run into him again tonight. I call him Autistic Man. At one time he was a nerd, a geek, a freak in his own manner. Now he is beyond all that. I find him sitting beside some skeletons of American cars that must be more than a century old. He has made for himself a tangle of various colored cables from which he gets enough light to read the latest issue of *Wired* magazine. I gesture hello to him and keep walking. Someone should make a documentary about him.

A mysteriously open container. I shine a match on the metal door. A whole bunch of stickers that say: SNACK CULTURE. Outside, on each end, in even bigger letters, it probably says the same thing: SNACK CULTURE. Inside there is a corpse (there has to be).

"Anything else?" asks Autistic Man.

"Tons of boxes, boxes, boxes."

"I mean, are there any other bodies?"

"You and I are here, right?"

"Other bodies. Other bodies."

He is almost asking me for them. I tell him:

"I don't know why there'd be any."

A helicopter patrol crosses in front of the moon. When they disappear, Autistic Man stares at me with his expressionless face and says:

"It's always the same. You, me, and a dead woman."

Dressed like a queen, or like a whore dressed like a queen, with a gown and sharp heels and a Vuitton purse, even the blood beneath her turns out to be an expensive puddle.

She had gotten dressed to go out with someone, maybe to a red carpet, maybe a party for the rich and famous, something that definitely went wrong. Her hair is messed up, make-up intact. She's not a young woman. She's past her forties but still maintains some traces of being a plastic girl. She has jewels, but no money. She surely had many friends and unpredictable lovers. You can infer all sorts of stories just by looking at her sprawled on the floor of the container. Of course, it's Vida G. The Cuban-American model, singer, actress... Her face still pretends to be unmistakable.

"We've got to do something. Let's find a phone," I suggest. "Let's find a damn phone. Let's go to Nokia, that little city in Finland."

But we don't move. We begin to argue about whether one of us should stay and take care of Vida's corpse (maybe examine it closely). And in the middle of that necrophilic argument the mist reaches us. The mist we hadn't realized was moving toward us.

For a moment, when it's almost grazing our noses, this is what we see: What seemed like a veil of water is like a front of electronic ether, a static-filled screen, a crystal that liquefies the landscape we see through it. It quickly passes over us and provokes no sensation at all; in any case the effect vanishes in a moment and in its wake everything remains the same as before, though slightly more illuminated and in various shades of grey.

Autistic Man and I look at each other. Autistic Man says he knows where to find a stretcher. I think: The only place that hospital junkyard exists is in his mind.

We place the dead Cuban-American in a metal stretcher with wheels, and roll down to the checkpoint that guards the zone. The guard comes out and shines a flashlight on us:

"Stop there! Who are you?"

We don't answer that question.

Theory of reflective silence.

"How'd you get in here?"

"We've always been inside," says Autistic Man.

"What are you carrying?" The guard comes closer to inspect the stretcher. "People come here to steal construction material, and you..."

"Do you recognize who it is?" I ask him. "Look closely."

He focuses his glance. He's fat, pathetic, about ten destroyed years older than Vida, and seems to need, at the very least, some eyeglasses.

"Such a delicious cougar," he admits. "It's obvious she's a capricious devil. Things like this are what make my heart suffer."

"The heart magazines come with waiting lists for transplants," says Autistic Man for no specific reason. "You have to read all types of things."

The guard looks at him with a mixture of confusion and reverence.

"Hey, I'm on a waiting list for transplants."

"So what are you doing here?" I ask him.

"I'm waiting for them to finish the freeway. The pay is shit, but they pay. I was a colonel in the Armed Forces, did you know that? And look where I've ended up. At a checkpoint watching TV all night." The guard looks at the corpse again, cracks his fingers. "Now I know! She's the one from the newscast."

We enter the checkpoint. The National Television Newscast is playing on a portable black & white TV, and there she is. Live and alive. Vida G is the main female newscaster. With devastating cleavage, she tells us about a tidal wave in Asia. But she's also the main male newscaster. Vida G with a thick mustache, her hair pulled up under a wig, her breasts flattened and invisible under a suit and tie. And she's also the weatherwoman: Wearing another suit, with different, tighter pants, the same voice moves a hand across the map, pointing out high temperatures.

And up next is Vida G as the smart young sportscaster who chats with a greying baseball analyst who is also her. And then Vida G in the cultural section: Her face rounder, a wide smile, disappointing blouse. And Vida G the newscaster who presents the features by Vida G, the correspondent who reports from all over the world. Go ahead, Vida. Thank you.

"This means something," the guard says.

His eyes grow wide and his face pale. He has seen a clear sign in the superimposition of so many news images with the body we've just found. This surely has to do with him; lately all the guns point in his direction. He was waiting for her, she's finally come to find him. The fatal hour is at hand. (But something else comes to mind for me.)

"Maybe it's not what you imagine. Without wanting to detract from your terminal conjectures, with the utmost respect, I think it could actually be quite the opposite. It could be an opportunity to have a new heart."

The guard blinks, perplexed.

"Her heart? To put on her heart?"

"Right now, before it gets cold. If what you say is true, you don't have anything to lose. On the other hand, if everything works out..."

"But how am I going to live with a woman's heart!"

"If women can, colonel, why can't you?"

He remains silent. Pensive, he puts his hand on his chest and taps it a few times.

Autistic Man and I look at each other. Autistic Man tells me he knows where to find a stretcher.

I think: He won't dare. I'm sure.

And yet, he lies down without hesitation on a metal stretcher beside Vida's and closes his eyes and acts like he has made a decision and more than that, as though he were anesthetized.

"Scalpel," I tell Autistic Man.

I try to concentrate, staring fixedly at the donor. I tear the dress's fabric. Of course she's not wearing a bra. I move her left breast slightly to the side. If I puncture the wrong spot a stream of silicone might leak out, I could find a stray bullet or a wad of bills, anything could happen. I make the incision. I open her up. I dig deeper. (I'll probably have to use a saw.) I pull apart the ribs and the plastic. Now I separate everything that's not important. The heart is left visible. I cut all the tubes and cables that hold it. I stick my dirty hands into the still-warm chest that keeps getting warmer...

It burns. (A perfumed smoke rises.) I pull out Vida G's heart.

"How disgusting," Autistic Man says at my back.

I hold Vida G's heart as though it were the most fragile thing in the world. It's moist. It's small and feminine. It's an erotic toy. It's got batteries: It vibrates in my hands, or maybe it is my nerves that are transmitting electricity into it.

Suddenly the heart beats. A single pulse. A strong pulse. I turn toward Autistic Man.

"Did you see that?"

"No."

I watch the heart for a few seconds. It doesn't beat again. I squeeze it a little. Nothing. I ask Autistic Man to hold it and I pick the scalpel up once more.

"Don't let it fall. Hand it over to me when I tell you."

"Why would I want to keep this? She doesn't mean anything to me."

"That's right."

I approach the other body. He has already taken off his uniform shirt and displays his flaccid, sunken chest, with a few solitary hairs that look like twisting worms. I feel a heart, my own, beating strongly. I look at Autistic Man, I look at the heart, that piece of woman in his hands. I look at the chest that's about to be opened. I lift the scalpel. I let it fall. I step back.

"I'm sorry, colonel."

He gets up. He starts to button up his shirt.

"I knew you wouldn't dare," he says.

Or maybe I will.

The colonel lies down without hesitation on a metal stretcher beside Vida's and closes his eyes and acts like he has made a decision and more than that, as though he were anesthetized.

"Scalpel," I tell Autistic Man.

1. I open her chest, take out the heart.

2. I open his chest, take out the heart.

I toss heart number 2 in the trash. I put heart number 1 inside him.

I close his chest while Autistic Man closes her chest.

"She means nothing to me," he murmurs, "and yet here I am filling a hole with freeway sand. She means nothing to me, and yet here I am sewing up her damaged body with wire."

I tell him to shut up, because, after all, he's the only one who understands what he's trying to say. That's one of the reasons I call him Autistic Man.

The military operation finally ends.

"Ready, colonel."

He gets up. He starts to button his shirt.

"Now let's bury that bitch," he says.

He doesn't need to call the cops anymore: Now he is the police. He tells us about other buried bodies, of a place he knows about, where people go (not the guys who pay shit—the guys who really pay you) to get rid of bodies at night.

Prostitutes. Beggars. Witnesses. And bodies the helicopters toss, as well, and desperate fugitives that bury themselves, digging with their fingernails. Corpses nobody will ever find, the colonel assures us. All this, as far as the eye can see, will soon be covered by tons of asphalt. All of it.

The three of us walk in silence. Leading Vida G's stretcher through dirt trails full of pebbles. We pass by trucks with immense wheels, we edge along giant deposits of water or cement. You can see even further: The reach of a satellite's images, future Google maps. I think of the infinite rails that depart from the nearby continent, an infinity of shining lights in the nightmare of concrete that approaches, roaring through the sea. It will pass over this strip of deserted land and keep going, heading south, toward the sea again.

The colonel looks around in the bushes, beneath some planks, and a pick and shovel appear under the light of the moon. Those are the only tools we need to hide the transplant. The true and definitive evidence of the transplant.

The colonel shows me his chest. The wound is an inflamed incision, of reddish color, crossed by a stitching of wires about to burst.

"Isn't this botched job proof enough?"

"No," I tell him. And I know I'm right.

"Shut up. Let's dig the hole."

We dig. The colonel digs with passion, with pride, with brutality. He deploys an otherworldly energy.

We stop at an acceptable depth. The colonel carries Vida G and drops her at the edge of the hole.

"Does anyone want to say a few words?"

I shrug my shoulders. I don't even know who she is. It would be best to speak of a theory. Or contradict it. But I don't say anything. (Vida's Life: From Havana to New Jersey to half the world's swollen ocular globes at the speed of those American cars that never stop on their way back to Havana once again and forever and...)

Autistic Man, as if he didn't want anyone else to hear him:

"No one will know where to find you anymore, Vida Google."

"G," I correct him pointlessly.

The colonel lifts his hand:

"Well I do have a few words. What I have to say is the following," he unbuckles his belt, opens his fly, pulls down his pants and his ragged underwear. He lifts Vida's dress, takes off her lace panties, throws them to the bottom of the hole. "Even though she's dead, this bitch is gonna know what a Cuban stud is."

The colonel's hand starts to negotiate an erection.

"I don't think it's the time," I tell him.

Autistic Man touches my shoulder and hands me a magazine. It's the issue of *Playboy* with Vida on the cover and in the centerfold pages. I really don't know where he gets these things.

"You'll see, you'll see..." kneeling and uncomfortable between Vida's open legs, the colonel fondles her closed chest, sucks on her bloody nipples, sticks his fingers in her vagina while he strokes his penis, stretches it, squeezes it...

It won't get hard.

I skim through the *Playboy*. The articles, the interviews, the fiction. I think of the places where those sticky pages have been read (and how they've been read, and by how many hands). Offices. Garages. Basements. Farms lost in the middle of remote roads. Nocturnal checkpoints throughout an entire journey amid ruins. The magazine had time to travel, from hand to hand, a long route until reaching Autistic Man, then me. It's an old issue, from years back.

"Let's go, colonel," I look up and observe him. "The moment has passed already."

"No, no... I can do it... now I can," and he keeps masturbating without a method and without pause, unable to achieve a decent erection. "She's gonna know that I can fuck her like anyone else," and with his trembling hand he presses his elusive glans against the dead lips of Vida's vagina, trying to make way. "I have her heart but I'm still... I'm still me, right?" He looks at me, at us. "Isn't that right?"

The colonel breathes with difficulty. Suddenly he stops touching his loins and pounds his chest forcefully. His face covered in sweat is paralyzed in a grimace. A scream of pain is cut short in his throat. It's just a few seconds before he falls on top of her like a dead animal.

I go up to him. I look for a pulse in his neck.

"A heart attack, or something like that," I conclude.

We push the corpses into the pit. Then we hear that noise that comes from afar and approaches, approaches, approaches more and more. Preceded by a noise of interference, the electronic mist reaches us again: The great screen looms over us and goes through us and keeps moving, leaving us with an altered shine and contrast. On mute. I'm about to start running.

"I think you should go watch the TV," Autistic Man tells me.

I run to the checkpoint. The National Television Newscast isn't over yet and gives no sign of ending any time soon.

The colonel speaks to the camera. The colonel is wearing discrete but efficient make-up, powder and eyelashes, his hair nicely set on his shoulders, real tits, fake earrings. The colonel is talking about a documentary that will soon be released; he reads with an affected voice, the prodigious phrase of insular engineering.

I turn the volume up. The colonel, wearing a perfect smile, announces they are now in contact with Vida G, who at this moment is in...

I back away, stumble on a chair, leave. "Go ahead, Vida."

I see her, microphone in hand, coming toward me. There are no cameras, or I can't see them. Nor can I tell where so much light is coming from.

To my left, suspended in the air at the height of my arm, is the logo of the Newscast beside the luminous letters that say LIVE. She walks dragging her high heels, one of them twisted and the other absent. Her dress and her arms are covered with coagulated dirt. Her eyes are two opaque crystal beads. She is transporting cockroaches and flies in her hair. Her entire body gives the impression of being full of holes through which things enter and exit.

Of course, I already know what she will ask me:

"Do you have anything to say about the construction of the freeway?"

Vida G puts the microphone in my face. I observe her bony hands, the nails that keep growing, unpainted and broken. The perfume becomes intense.

"Nothing else," I answer.

But I could just as well add any other phrase. Besides, no one is going to understand what I'm trying to say.

17 Abstracts of a Notebook's Entries

Story by Polina Martínez Shviétsova

Translated by David Iaconangelo

1.

Double-nationality hybridity. Survivors without context or ontology. Tepid waters between the fire of being and the ice of nothingness. Poetry's infinite foam in the middle of the desert. Pamyla, protagonist.

2.

I'm riding in an old American truck and I wonder, "What will I feel after I make love?"

We're headed toward central Hershey. Not the one in Pennsylvania, but rather the twin brother built here, the Camilo Cienfuegos. I'm carrying my notebook along with my backpack-home, which today doesn't weigh so heavily. I'm granting myself a day to think less and try to be a normal person. Though I can't help but wonder, "What will I feel after I make love?"

3.

I'm riding in an old Russian truck and I don't wonder anything anymore.

All around me, the great patriotic march of June 13: The people cry out in support of a constitutional reform. The pain is plain and honest. The isolation, the poetry of my little fantastic tales which I try to work out but can't tell right, the delirium: All of it put down in this notebook, pale testimony to the adventures of a Slavic girl on an island of frozen fire, where I gather up the remains of its dead nature with bovine mushrooms.

The world tastes like recycled plastic and I'm a fried patty of sun, *cruxified* on the purity which leads to forgetting, annunciation of death. It can't be easy to shout about virtues when the pot keeps turning the soya mince into steam. And without any money. None. Not a damn cent. Where did I put my shawl with Arabic scrawling soaked in *Eau de Cannabis?*

I believe it was Cortázar who spoke of a "poetics of sponges and chameleons." I put that down. Sponge: Figure of minute and fragmentary porosity, of an interstitial nature. Chameleon: Figure of confusion, *caosmos*, and otherness dating back to unknown ages. Of a medieval nature.

4.

"Hey, Vlady! Finally catching you awake."

"Stop fussing around and get in, Pamyla."

A cassette of Slavic music: *Zolotoe koltso*. And everything was in a wonderful heap, circles of gold and clouds of green pyramidal smoke.

"Hey, weren't you saying you didn't like the name Brandy as a person in my stories? Well, I'm thinking I'll change it up for Whiskey instead, how's that?"

"Nah, homie, I can't get down with Whiskey either. Make me Vodka, it's stronger and not so hard on the *pieschien*."

"You sure about that? Whiskey's the best."

"Shit, you can get vodka up to 99 proof. In Russia the peasants used to make it out of rotten potatoes, and they'd get loaded off of it to pick faster and ferment more of it again."

"*Da, da*. They drink to eat and eat to drink. Alright, Vlady, I got you. I'll make you Vodka in all the stories I'm going to write."

"You should make me Stepan Razin, the rebel, instead. Or the soldier Suvorov. Or general Kutuzov. Or Vlasov. Homie, what you know about any of them?

5.

"Hey, you all are halfies?"

I address the group timidly, but with light-hearted defiance. We're in Tarará, where the Ukrainian Embassy has organized a buffet. One of them turns 180 degrees and quips:

"And who the *bliat* are you?"

"I'm me, Pamyla Shvietsova. Ask your mother about me. And you?"

But the ambassador has already picked the microphone back up and is urging us to pray and toast.

Afterward we fill our plates with delicious imported sandwiches. I also serve myself a cuba libre while I return the gaze of everyone eating and drinking in the group around me, my attacker included.

At the end, they repeated from start to finish the national anthems of both countries before a voice we all recognized sounded through the speakers:

...*naplisya ya pianiym, tepier ya pianim ne doido ya... do doma napilsya ya... piamiyn tepier... ne doidu ya do doma...*

It went on like that until midnight. The lost songs of Vladimir Vysotsky, Viktor Tsoi, and even the Town Musicians of Bremen. All of it brilliant and surreal as could be.

"You're my psychopath matryoshka, you're my psychopath matryoshka," the guy who attacked me keeps repeating, inexplicably.

We got to be great friends later. Almost lovers. Later, great enemies. Almost lovers, too.

"Little Snow Bear," I called him in both cases, because his name ended up being Misha.

It's the "Slavic soul," I guess. I scribble that down in my notebook, in forgotten Cyrillic characters.

6.

Everyone watches me fall into an unexpected trance. I howl with laughter. My hands are sweating and so is the rest of my body. I feel like wriggling out of my clothes, my memory and my feelings.

I sense a new germ of something, a surge of something unreal, an ecstasy. I must write everything down at once. Someone dictates it to me from the very back of my head:

"I see a painting where the components are: Pamyla, me + Caluff, the Lebanese + Pasha, the Russian. The painting acquires a virtual dimension and, more than color, I sense the magnitude of what's occurring to us. Me, trapped between them. Naked. I'm in the habit of stripping down wherever. The naked Lebanese presses forward with all his weight over my face, my neck, down to my breasts. He absorbs them and draws with his tongue the figure I imagine in them. He scratches my skin with fingers like obscene tiger claws, while I scream and his braid penetrates into my shell. I see the sleep slipping from his eyes like a gust of spirit. Behind me is Pasha, with his fleshy-lipped mouth, tongue-kissing the back of my neck, my shoulders and the whole length of my back. The refinement of his manhood mingles with a touch of roughness. A moan slips from me and he drives his braid into my darkest rose, wet between my two mountains of snow-white flesh. I moan as their two braids work into my voluptuous body like serpents of smoke, the paths they forge in me are unique. The milk and honey they gush perfumes me. The night's echo is incense letting off a fog of seaweed. Only we are love made into a universe within life, in body and soul. I award them a kind of violet thunderclap, the crash of snow and desert: it's like a veil, mist or vapor...

Then they hold me, in a hopeless gesture that can't be emptied of nostalgia. That's why I look for magic in the twilight, in any other place I can. "Life is elsewhere," I think—the metaphor that isn't Kundera's—and I jot it down. I also write down, "the poetic memory of the loved one." And then I write gratefully for letting me clear up the meaning of my last doubt.

Over the speakers, Moonspell penetrates me with a "Tenebrarum Oratorium" from his "Erotic Compemdyum."

In the dictionary, the word "erotic" doesn't have an etymology, its *onlysignifichaos*: A flute made of an exile's tibia whose notes wield their weeping in silence; a dance through space playing a skin drum of freedom; resurrection's sonorous synonym.

"Pamy, you alright? Your pressure go down yet?" one says to me from the blank page.

It's one of my inventions, though I can't make out which.

7.

Pamyla, a thawout. Cross section of those innards called the soul. Lobotomy. Opening holes in characters. Slicing out random moments, exploits, solitary rooms on this side of the ocean, and the bitter taste of countries and their smells: Question-less answers and not vice versa. An endlessness. An ending of colors rung out by talking heads, masters and messiahs who never accepted its gory reality.

8.

"I was going to make a sketch of God but the ink got thrown out," I say to myself as I weep in the darkness, and I'm not dancing.

I'm blind, like Björk. And I'm missing a lead zeppelin's hoarse voice of Led Zeppelin in "Since I've Been Loving You." And I'm missing Igor. So I remember him from a distance. He was a winged *kniaz*, with a bicycle and a guitar, a Bremen musician trapped beneath an endless sun.

He would always come with his levity, his Dante Aligieri-style profile, the Son of God in his eyes, one of Lermontov's angels. Igor broke off from the Real. A little hawk impossible not to adore. The opposite of beauty isn't ugliness. The dictionary is a useless weapon when it comes to writing. Choosing a shit-less beauty is like playing in a world of kitsch, practically an instrument for vociferating to the masses. But vociferate what? Only ugliness born of the soul and turned into creation must be authentic. Only Igor is.

"Not all in Heaven have I hated; not everything on earth have I despised." Pushkin's pronouncement is like the announcing of Igor's tragic destiny.

The promise broken like a pane of glass. The discovery of an enormous knife with a medieval hilt, to put to the test the very heart of our dedication. My panic, and his terrible and sudden resolution, evaporating amid the pot being inhaled and a 1972 plastic disk —"Since I've Been Loving You"—my voice hoarse as that of the girl then named Robert Plant and now Björk. An era whose time was exhausted for us in a single chord.

"I was going to throw out the ink and ended up with God," I tell myself, dry-faced in the darkness, and now I am dancing.

9.

"Zionist, murderer, criminal, dumbass, *pridurka*: You really botched things up, you really dropped the ball!" Fedia said in the dream, grabbing me by the neck.

"Where'd you learn to call people things like that?" was the only thing that occurred to me to say.

I woke up, and even a long time later it was as if Fedia hadn't died. As if her body wasn't still dangling from the noose, a watch without hands or time.

10.

"Man, if Dostoevsky was here," Dima says, laughing in my face, "humanity would be lost."

"Even more lost?" I say soberly.

"And that's no two-kopek Russian drama. Not one of these remakes of Tarkovsky done by the ICAIC. Not the Stanislavsky method applied to national folklore. Not Mayakovsky's dead body with its bloodstained CCCP passport. Not Trotsky's death as told by Sudoplatov. Not the Kremlin towers felled by an American Airlines Boeing 9/11."

"So," I retort, irritated, "what the fuck is...?"

Dima just stays quiet. He's pure theory, he never has his feet on the zemlya: At times he reminds me of Fedia's final dance.

11.

Idea I: In a public bathroom, the "cold, turbid and gentle" waters lap at our knees.

Idea II: The contaminated waters where condoms and lumps of shit float, with traces of blood and black clots like loaves of bread.

Idea III: A piece of bread open like a heart in the midst of an attack, the map of every Russia clipped short inside and eaten by an ant-lion named Piotr.

12.

Sleeping at the foot of the oil lamp again. It's my magic helper, as Fromm might've put it. Once again the simultaneity makes me feel like a volley ball in a pre-Olympic game between Cuba and the USSR, with the Atlantic Ocean and the whole twentieth century lost in the nets. Once again the perpetual discontinuous line, telling me that on the cover of my first and only book, *Skizein*, Pushkin will sit between John Lenin and Vladimir Ilich Lennon in the park on 15th and 6th, with the worst *pajmelia* of his life and still shooting off about art, philosophy, and civil society. Once again I'm sleepless at the foot of the oil lamp, writing everything down just in case.

13.

Listening with headphones to the band Antiloop, the great-grandchildren of Moby Dick: I'm tired and starving. Gone. My eyes wander amid the crowd and meet Ilya's gaze. She realizes I'm in a state of coma and wraps me up between arms made of birch wood, a smile flowering on her face as if we didn't actually hate each other.

She tells me that I was part of a crazy déjà-vu moment of

hers. She saw me just then like a serpent or something amphibious or nostalgic. Then she shows me a photo of Anna, the writer who dedicated one of her books to me with: "I will barge into your soul without a name tag."

I don't understand the full meaning of the scene: Antiloop, Herman Melville, Ilya, the birch trees, Anna, is it possible to be born again, but for the first time? How not to always have to be returning, without first having procured passage? Among those who haven't yet been born, who will know how to read me?

14.

At the movies they're showing *Good-Bye, Lenin*, a German film. From the seats, we hear Misha the Bear shouting himself hoarse. He might as well be in Moscow Olympic Stadium. He's ecstatic, for some reason. The usherette shines her flashlight on him and threatens to expel him.

Misha curses her in Russian and, also in Russian, threatens to burn down that fucking theater if he's not left alone.

"Mir, mir, mir, mir, mir, mir, mir," he repeats in a falsetto.

The usherette smiles and heads off. She's letting him rest in mir: She must think he's just a little bastard. Misha keeps quiet now, with Lenin's head flying in a helicopter from Berlin to the short-sighted lenses of his glasses. He makes faces. No one in the group notices, but I know he's acting ecstatic so as not to break down in tears.

"Good-bye, Misha," I wrote that night in my notebook.

15.

Idea IV: The mirror watches us and tells us we "look like newlyweds all naked like this." The mirror refracts our image. It shouts at us like Moses at the Jews, "We can't hear you, because He flows down from his pedestal, with his renewed sight, back from death." As for me, I'm the *AuTorah*, the authority who wrote The Old Testament and afterward three times denounced it.

Idea V: A crow flies, denying us the essence written in the Tablets of Stone. It crushes us with falling meprobamates, from which hang our destiny like a desert: Motionless, errant landlessness. There's a strict cat sleeping on my roof. I circle back to the flames of infancy and I'm a disciple of Freud, Lacan, Deleuze, alternated with Pasha, Igor, Dima, Vlady, and the Lebanese.

Idea VI: I gather up my horseshoe-less steeds. The horses stamp on the winter vases of the Ermitage. It's the blood on which I feed the ghetto where the breeze or brume or crack of dreams of a gothic intellectuality lives. The Aurora Cruiser fires cannon shots at nine at night. Sofia's tomb lies in an apocryphal cellar in the Cathedral of Havana. My insides get worn out with the sacred torture. Now I prepare myself and kiss the cross of rustic wood. It's a bad day for whoever's just a word in the desert and the lashes pierce the abyss. The blank paper fits in my lungs and there's no first reason to begin to narrate. I say nothing.

16.

I'm riding in an old Cuban truck and the driver asks, without looking at me, "Why don't you touch it? If you touch it for me, I'll give you a hundred rubles."

He drives with one hand, his left. With the right he shows me his dick. It's broad daylight and we're going down Calle 26. When we reach Zapata, we turn off. The cemetery passes us on the other side of the windows. Farther down, the modern, inhabited buildings and the pyramidal monolith of the Plaza. It's like a movie. I assume it is.

The driver's phallus recalls the 180 meters of chimney of a thermoelectric plant to the north of Havana, rising up like a flagless pole, facing the sea. The guy has an ugly penis, just like him. But together they're beautiful.

I don't respond. He doesn't insist. We approach a stoplight and I see him cover himself with his shirt. He leans toward me. I let him. He whispers something in my ear and extends his card of introduction.

I read it quickly. It's from Sovexportfilm, a fake business. No doubt about it, we live in a Russian movie. Whether it's a story of war or love, I don't know. Either way, at the light I shoot out the door without saying goodbye.

At the end, the son of the bitch seemed to me like a poor guy. In the end, if he really would have paid me, between the shame and disgust, I might've been able to touch it for him.

17.

Drunkenness of non-nationality. Sur-die-ors of the hyperlink and ideology. Social-ipsists rowing on an iceberg which resembles a caiman. Volcanic waters or cesspools seeking to regurgitate themselves into the sea. Short-circuit or voltaic spark between two chromosomes in black and white. The soul of a slave, the soul of a libertine: Steppenwolf. Cutup of images. Flea market of images. Hour zero of narration. The insipid and painless of any double country: Question-less answers and not vice versa. 17 out-of-focus snapshots. 17 abstracts of an agenda. 17 springtimes broken from the single blow of a hurled stone and no shard ever called Pamyla: The agony of a protagonist. Curtain...

Glossary

Zolotoe koltso: Gold ring

Pieschien: Liver

Naplisya ya pianiym, tepier ya pianim ne doido ya... do doma napilsya ya... piamiyn tepier... ne doidu ya do doma: I've drunk enough now, now I'm really drunk, now I won't make it home...

Pridurka: Moron, idiot

Kopeks: Cents

Pajmelia: Hangover

The Same Eyes

Story by Lizabel Mónica

Translated by David Iaconangelo

*Then you turned toward the mirror, to the image of your face
reflected there in the murky surface, to prove your existence.
No longer did you recognize yourself. You were the other
woman, dressed in an outmoded nurse's uniform.*
Farabeuf
—Salvador Elizondo

And then the last of them: Denisse, from the waist up. I was seventeen, and I hadn't seen that photo since I was a girl. I had been entrusted with it as with her eyes—now mine too—and the old suitcase I hadn't opened in ten years.

She was pretty. That blouse always looked good on her. But her favorite was the white one with red flowers around the neckline, over her breasts, almost over her areolas, which I could make out when I saw her dressed.

There were her crooked lips, painted red. Her blank eyes. Underneath those eyes you could make out the clean tongue, the even teeth. A mouth not made for talking.

Denisse was laconic. She would reserve verbal communication for moments when there was no other solution, like on that night when, perhaps convinced of the contrary, she said, "Don't worry, honey, I'm sure nothing's going to happen to us."

Then the clacking of the metal knocker sounded at the door. Startled, I dropped the photo album next to my feet.

I bent to pick it up before going to the door. It had to be Lilian.

***

"Since I was six, there's been two types of doors to me. The ones that make me sick with nerves and give me this harsh pain in my stomach, and the ones that don't. The first smell like glue; the second like all kinds of things, or they don't have any... wait, no, it went out, give me a light."

I reached out toward Nara, but before she could react,

Sandra lifted her lighter and helped me relight the joint. I smoked some more.

Soon, I didn't feel like chatting anymore, and I rubbed my fingers together as if to demand something. Maybe I was only trying to palpate my sudden desire not to speak another single word for the moment. I passed the joint.

"Hey, hello over there, girl."

They were all looking at me, and Nara was waving her hand.

I must have been absorbed in my fingers for some time. With marijuana, one loses notions of temporality. In any case, whether twenty minutes or a second had passed, I still didn't feel like talking, and worse, I didn't want to be there anymore.

It was a sign that something was going to happen... Maybe I was already remembering it.

***

My father was awake. He wanted to know what I'd been doing, where I'd been. I told him at Nara's house and that I was going to sleep. He grabbed my arm and though he didn't say anything, I knew he'd seen the marijuana in my eyes. He let me realize that he knew. Then he let me go and told me to call him next time to say where I was.

***

I went to my room but couldn't get to sleep right away. I thought about Denisse. I heard my father turn off the lights and, as always, open the door to the balcony before he went to bed. I thought of the knife he kept at his bedside to defend against thieves.

Then I imagined my father entering the room. He never did that without asking permission from the other side of the curtain.

It was a very strange thought.

Finally I went to sleep.

***

The next day my father woke up in a bad mood, and I don't remember why we argued. We ended up unusually irritated with each other. Accustomed to talking as little as possible, we would almost always avoid fighting. On rare occasions we would lose control; that day was one of those occasions.

I shouted at him without looking him in the eye, raising my voice in a way I'd never dared to before. I knew he was too angry with me to hold back.

"Clean up the kitchen," he said, yanking me up off the chair.

Maybe I should've stayed quiet. But that day I wasn't in the mood to repress what I felt, maybe because of the aftereffects of the marijuana, or because at one point or another I'd have to go to school; what's certain is I couldn't hold back. I told my fears to go to hell and squared up to him.

"As soon as you get out of here," I said.

I'd never used the informal address with him to his face. He stayed quiet a moment. Then he brought his face up close to mine and said quietly, but pronouncing the words slowly, hoarsely, with a harsh tone he knew how to use well:

"You get more like Denisse every day. If you're not careful, you'll end up like her."

His disgusting face was right up to mine, and I couldn't move. When he spoke again, his breath shot out on top of me:

"The same black eyes..."

We stayed like that for a few seconds I thought would never end, until he moved away slowly, without taking his eyes off me.

I spun away and went outside. He tried to stop me but couldn't. I slammed the door and bolted away, afraid he might come after me. I kept running until I was out of sight of the house.

I wasn't going to go to school.

I went to see Sandro. I wanted him.

***

"Want to be by yourself?"

I don't know, I thought, how should I know? Sandro was waiting for a response.

"No."

"Can I ask you what happened?"

I didn't look at him. I didn't feel like answering.

"I think it was when I put you face down, maybe you didn't like it when I flipped you over or I was too rough, maybe I should've asked you."

"Do you always have to know everything?"

"I'd like to keep on seeing you."

"We see each other every day at Nara's house."

"I'd like to be closer to you."

"It's too hot."

"What?"

"Having someone too close to me suffocates me."

"Is this okay?"

"A little more that way... Actually, I'll sit here and you stay on the bed."

I started to get dressed. I felt awkward and didn't feel like talking.

"I'm leaving."

"Wait, don't you want to go for a walk? Mairet!"

I heard him yell something as I was closing the door. I think it was "See you at Nara's house?"

***

When I got home, my father wasn't there, like every Monday. Lilian would get there in an hour.

Mondays were the best days, my special days with Lilian, but that Monday I felt anxious.

I'd stolen Sandro's cigarettes. I lit one and sat down on the bed. I thought I should go into my father's room before Lilian got there to see if it was neat and to put up the mirrors, but I didn't feel like going in there just then.

I put down the cigarette. I was too anxious to smoke. I didn't want to have anything in my hands.

I thought of Denisse, then suddenly thought of Denisse again. A few minutes later I was opening the old suitcase.

I wasn't sure if I wanted to do it or not, but there I was doing it, and I was too agitated to reflect on what I was doing. There were the photos, swaddled up in old clothes.

The first pages of the album were for the "uncles." Each one bearing the curious names she'd given them: Uncle Carlos, Uncle Pablo, Uncle Justino, Uncle González, Uncle Alberto, Uncle Federico... a long succession of men who only had a smiling face and Denisse's neatly handwritten caption in common. They occupied most of what anyone would stupidly call family memories.

And after the final uncle, my father, with his face closed and fierce.

I looked in the pack; there weren't any cigarettes left and I badly wanted a cigarette.

I returned to the album. There was the last photo: Denisse.

***

After I picked the album off the floor, I went to open the door.

It was Lilian. I saw her inexpressive mouth through the grille. A mouth that always reminded me of another mouth.

When I opened the grille door, I knew I was going to find Lilian's inert mouth and right then see another mouth, one with crooked lips... It was the mouth, her mouth, Denisse's mouth, and the legs coming in behind the smell of glue as the door closed behind them both. Those legs were like Denisse's when she would put on a skirt because she was about to go out. "Today's a good day for work, honey." She didn't say anything else, but I knew it was one of those unpleasant afternoons when she gave me her back.

Lilian smiled. I looked her in her grey eyes and saw my eyes, my black eyes in them.

Lilian walked toward my father's room, and I hurried after her to watch how she got undressed. Lilian would always move quick and leave me alone there in the living room. *I don't want to be alone today, Denisse, don't go...*

By the time I entered the room Lilian was already naked. Her clothes were tossed on the nightstand, covering my father's portrait, only his blue eyes visible beneath Lilian's skirt.

Now I had to get undressed too. I wasn't alone long. Denisse came back afterward, making a rough-day face: "The men are being such a pain today."

Lilian looked at me and I understood she was waiting for me to take off my clothes. As always, I went toward the mirror, Denisse undressed, I saw her breasts, her ass, her long hair, the strange way she was observing me. Someone knocked hard on the door. Denisse looked at me: "Don't worry, honey, I'm sure nothing's going to happen to us." She put on a skirt and the blouse, her areolas prominent and unhidden by a bra.

She went to the door. A man entered and plunked down a bottle. Lilian came over and stroked me for a few seconds. She knelt to lick between my legs. Feeling her wet nose in my vagina for a moment made me forget that afternoon I'd just been remembering, but she got up and looked at me again, with her grey eyes, and as always, even if I couldn't pin it down before, with Denisse's black eyes.

Denisse looked angry: "Get out of here! No men are allowed in my house." He hadn't seen me. I was in the corner of the room, the corner Denisse had assigned me to before opening the door. "Señora," he murmured, and threw himself at Denisse, seeking her lips with his own. Irritated, Denisse looked at me, went speechless, and tried to push the man out of the apartment.

Lilian blinked, disconcerted, knowing she couldn't ask what was happening to me; I'd asked her never to speak when we arranged to see other like this. I struck her, and she took that as a sign that everything had gone back to normal, that what we usually did was about to begin.

She returned the blow and shoved me back against one of the mirrors. The man pushed Denisse inside and shut the door. He threw her down on the bed. Denisse looked at me from the mirror. He'd laid down on top of her.

"Wait," she said. "The girl." He moved to the side, Denisse sat up and took me by the hand, led me to the bathtub, said, "Stay here; if you stay quiet he'll leave soon," and closed the bathroom door, which smelled of glue.

I turned around, grabbed Lilian, and kissed her violently. I squeezed the flesh of her shoulders. Lilian separated herself from me. She pinned me against the wall and ran her tongue along my mouth, over my face, as if she wanted to swallow my eyes. I clung to the wall until one of my nails ripped off. I forgot myself, in order to withstand the pain.

I opened the bathroom door. I'd always listened to her, but not that day; I don't know if it was out of curiosity or fear of being by myself. The smacks I gave Lilian made her back up. She couldn't do much but howl, and I got really turned on.

I left the bathroom and walked slowly, so they wouldn't hear me. I reached the room and saw them. Him on top of her, moving. Denisse's face turned back to face the door. Lilian had grabbed me by the hair and the two of us fell to the floor, our bodies rolling over one another.

Lilian, out of breath and with bloodshot eyes, got up and went to look for the knife my father kept at his bedside. I squeezed my nipples as I waited. He had picked up Denisse to put her on all fours on the bed, her ass facing him. For the first time I was seeing that which I'd only seen in the magazines Denisse hid under her mattress. I watched them, but her face was still turned towards the door. I wanted to see her eyes and her mouth. Lilian was on top of me, offering me the knife.

I went toward Denisse until I could see her face. I stopped in front of her. Her gaze fell beyond me. Her eyes were blank. She saw me, shouted at me, but I couldn't move. I didn't know what to do and froze there, watching her. Lilian offered me her arm, her mouth open and full of saliva. Her eyes restless.

There were Denisse's eyes, as she shouted and tried to sit up. She struck at the man, who tried to catch her hands as she fought to be able to get up. He grabbed her legs and pulled them toward him; the pull made Denisse lose control of her hands, and her head fell hard against the floor.

I sank the knife into where there weren't any marks and cut the veins. Lilian moved her arm so that the blood streamed over her body, turning her vagina red; I penetrated her with my red hands. Denisse didn't move. I drank the blood from Lilian's arm. Only Denisse's ass was moving. He jiggled it, holding her by the hips. When he saw, he let her fall on the bed and looked at me. I ran to the bathroom and closed the door. He tried to open it. I screamed at him, wept, fell asleep.

When they got me out Denisse wasn't on the bed anymore. They made me put my things in a suitcase and took me to my father, that man I'd only seen in the photo.

When we finished, like always, I got up and looked for the bandages Lilian would need. I carried her over into my father's bed. While she recuperated I cleaned the blood from her body. I contemplated her.

The truth is that seeing her limp and motionless body excited me so much, I wanted to touch her again. Softly, as soon as she woke up and opened her grey eyes, Denisee's black eyes were on me.

That Monday night, when Lilian left and I was alone once more, I took the album and put it inside the old suitcase, then took a shower.

I closed the door. Even if there wasn't anyone there, I closed the bathroom door. Getting out of the shower, I felt tired. I knew I wouldn't go to Nara's house that night.

I sat down on the tile floor and went to sleep.

Jumping into an Empty Pool

Story by Osdany Morales

Translated by Diana Álvarez-Amell

1

If this were a Woody Allen film, Ariel Costa thought, the evening he arrived in Santo Domingo, I would meet two women at two different bars.

I would vaguely fall in love with both. One would be American—an actress vacationing in the tropics. The other would fit the same description with the same three attributes. But the first would be blond, the second one brunette.

In short order I would marry the blond. Together we would fly out to Los Angeles. Her father would see something of himself in me, as he was years ago when he was younger, except for the part about me being Cuban. Stirred by the reflection of his own image, my father-in-law would arrange for me to meet with producers. They would acquire the screen rights to my short stories with the idea of turning them into blockbuster movies. I'd settle for an ocean-front home where I would write, all the while feeling inscrutably happy.

2

One morning, on the golf course, my father-in-law would introduce me to Orson Martinez. He is the ghostwriter who would adapt my stories into screenplays. Orson Martinez is French and spellbound by American movies. His successful screen adaptations have brought several stories to life and have spawned over seven sequels. Some even made it past a fourth prequel.

Orson Martinez's theory is that if you are French and so

taken with Hollywood movies, the best thing to do is move to California and start making films. The rest would take care of itself. I am clueless as to what "the rest" is, although my wife and her father seem to know. They both nod and then look at me.

Orson Martinez takes my book published by UNIÓN in Cuba. He waves good-bye from his convertible as he drives away with my book. He sends a text message to let me know he made it home but has yet to read my book. He sends a text message again after reading the first story and then another after the second story. After that there are no more texts. He shows up at my house in Los Angeles at exactly twelve past four. The pages of my book are all scribbled with notes. Although I don't quite get it, he found a movie somewhere in those stories.

My wife asks whether it has a role for her. It does. It is that of a woman whose son goes missing. She asks him whether it also has a role for her dear friend Jimmy. It does. He is the one who kidnaps the child, but that is to be revealed only towards the end of the movie. My wife squeals delightedly. She is torn between texting or phoning. She decides to call. Jimmy, she whispers on the phone, we have a screenplay. We both have parts. Jimmy's own squeals are heard on the other end of the line. It's Ariel's script. Wait until you read it. You'll be so excited you'll be jumping into an empty pool.

Orson Martinez turns his head and stares at her as if she had been, as it were, indiscreet. But no, he simply liked what he heard. In the margin of a page he jots down: JUMP-ING INTO AN EMPTY POOL.

I ask Orson Martinez which of my stories he wants to adapt. All of them, he tells me, every single one of them to be precise. Let's get this straight though, there is not going to be any "writer" character or mention of books either. The storyline that is to be patched together from the scraps of my stories that are originally all about writers goes more or less like this:

3

A woman—my wife—takes her three year-old son to an amusement park. A vendor hands him a fish-shaped balloon as a gift. The boy with the balloon rides the carousel. She stands by the merry-go-round snapping pictures of her son. In the split second when the boy is hidden from her view as the carousel rotates, she sees the inflated fish ascend. When the carousel turns around again, the seat where her son sat is now empty.

The fish floats above the park that begins to seem progressively smaller. This could mean that a high angle shot takes the fish's point of view. Or perhaps it is a metaphor for the impossibility that my wife will ever see her child again. She has a dear friend named Jimmy. She calls Jimmy to tell him her son was kidnapped because of that "thing with the father." She is convinced there can be no other explanation.

The police begin tracking down leads from the pictures she took that day. There isn't much time. Her husband is nowhere to be seen except in photographs. He disappeared years ago. A scientist, he had performed experiments on himself trying to have children. My wife conceived a child fathered by this now long gone scientist.

She gave birth to the child. But there was always something peculiar about the boy. By age three he stopped growing. He was a veritable genetic fountain of eternal youth. A lot of dangerous people were after him in hot pursuit. To escape from them she had to keep moving. Her life had become a never ending flight, always running away with her son in tow. And she senses she'll grow old just trying to rescue him because—can you imagine?—her son is going to be three forever.

4

On the film's opening night I would ask Orson Martinez what the boy not growing past his third birthday was all about. He would tell me that there were four plausible explanations:

1. It was a French nod and a wink to American films. 2. It was a distilled version of all the writers who show up in all of my stories. 3. It was Orson Martinez. 4. It was Ariel Costa himself.

For my sake, he would let me pick which it would be. Then I could go ahead and happily sign the screen rights to all the sequels and the prequels. That would make my job easier. Think about it, he ends up telling me, the kid is eternal. As long as you don't get off track, everything should come up roses.

Afterwards I would return home, trailing behind my wife. Once there, still in my tuxedo, I'll wonder, Ariel Costa thought, whatever happened to that brunette, the other actress I would have met at a bar one evening in Santo Domingo if this were a Woody Allen film?

Unfinished Business

Story by Erick Mota
Translated by Karen González

Nights in Old Havana are always loud. Each carrier rocket shakes the old rocks of the almost sunken buildings. The canals with black waters, which run across the archaic streets, light up with the gleam of oxygen and hydrogen in combustion. The water, mixed with petroleum from the old Soviet cargo boats, vibrates and flutters with every take-off. Like gigantic flares, the Protons-II rockets light up the old parts of the city with every departure. They bruise the sky of Autonomous Havana and disappear into the cosmos monopolized by the Russians.

Up there they have the space stations, the satellites with nuclear warheads, the servers for the Global Neural Network, the whole Russian way of life, as those balseros(i) in Florida say. Down here illegal immigrants sleep in the corridors at Almejeira hospital and work on the platforms in Underguater for four kopeks. All of them with the hope of getting into one of those rockets that will take them to the Romanenko station. Or any other. An entire life of sacrifice just to be like one of the Russians. Another tovarish.

But you know very well that that, more than a dream, is a fantasy. That the Russians never treat anyone like an equal. That you end up being another immigrant in another place. Another foreigner in a strange land.

You, too, became a victim of that fantasy. You lived in a city in chaos, after a hurricane sank everything and forced everybody to start shooting each other. You went up there and you never looked back.

Now the chaos is organized. There are abakuas(ii) pacifying Old Alamar, Santeros(iii) in Downtown, and

Babalawos(iv) in Vedado. Investors of religious corporations in Miramar, and the FULHA that watches over the old fortress in La Cabaña. FULHA: The emergent force that tried to make use of the army, police, and government, but in the end it just ended up becoming another force fighting in the midst of anarchy. Nobody rules over Havana. There is no order in this city. But, at least, there's less chaos.

And you came back. Not looking for order or chaos. You came back because you had no choice. Because there is no better place to be than home. And Havana, even if it's Hell, is your home.

You came down in one of the last landing capsules left. You fell in Puertohabana Bay thanks to the good aim of your Russians tovarish. You were rescued by the Marine Coast Guard. Last time you heard anything about them, they were a FULHA special unit. Now, who knows.

The FMC speedboat zigzagged through the street of Old Sunken Havana until it arrived at the Cathedral. There, in the space station pier, they left you in the hands of some guys from Russian customs. They finished the papers and offered a boat to Underguater or Vedado. You said no.

You are now legal in Autonomous Havana. When you left, you were a mere Cuban citizen. Now, you have a Russian passport that allows you to enter and leave this city-State that you barely recognize anymore.

You look at the ocean, the sunken buildings, the layer of petroleum that moves in unison with the water.

"Should I call you a cab, comrade?"

"A boatman that will take me to Sunken Cayo Hueso will be enough," you say while you give a ruble to the employee of the space station that rests over the old Cathedral, "and don't call me comrade. Please."

You take a twenty pesos motor boat. You go through the Underguater's stretch of canals until you get to Sunken Cayo Hueso. You look for an address. You find it. You give the boatman a ruble. He says he doesn't have change. You reply in a bad mood that you don't need it.

You take the half-sunken stairs up the building. The houses that are still habitable begin after the third floor. You remember this place. Too well.

Going up the stairs there are five boys. They're wearing t-shirts, they carry revolvers around their waists, and they smell like cheap vodka. Kids from the neighborhood that dream of becoming famous aseres one day: Bodyguards of famous porn stars from the studios at Old UCI or working for the santeros in Downtown Havana. They all want to be successful and become rich in the most mediocre and small-minded way possible.

You realize the neighborhood hasn't changed at all. You walk by them without paying much attention. One of them, the one who seems to be the leader, cuts in front of you.

"To pass by here, you have to pay a toll, dude."

"And why should I have to pay you, dude? I don't see you doing anything worth a single kopek."

"The problem is what I'm gonna do to you if you don't pay me."

The others laugh. To you it is just returning to the old neighborhood.

"Does your mom know you're here? You better go back home, dude. Before you hurt yourself with that gun."

The boy loses his composure. He's red in the face with anger. He yells, pushes you, aims his gun at you. Just what you want. You were always good at making people lose control.

You grab his wrist, you twist it. There is a shot and the bullet finds its target in the chest of another boy. In one stroke you break his elbow. The scream makes the others freeze. The boy bends in pain. With tenderness you take the gun and let down a blow with the handle into his head. The body falls unconsciously in the middle of a pool of blood.

"I already told you," you throw the gun away. "Go back to your houses. This isn't for you."

And you keep going up the stairs that leave you short of breath. You are old and used to the easy lifestyle of the orbit. You can't fight properly and go up four floors at the same time. The neighborhood hasn't changed, but you have.

When you finally arrive at the door, you're exhausted. You are almost too out of breath to call out. You don't want to do it either. You respond to the perverted need to suffer for those things. Especially for the past. But you have thought about that before. If you were able to control your instincts, you would have stayed in space. Living comfortably, with the Russians in zero gravity.

You knock on the door. She opens. Secretly, you were hoping she wouldn't be there, or that she wouldn't want to let you in.

"It's you. I never thought you'd come back."

"I never I thought I would. But here I am."

"Yes, here you are. That much I can tell."

She remains in an awkward silence for a few seconds. Then she walks away toward the window. She has no intention of closing the door in your face or yelling at you until you leave. She does not seem to have any intention of asking you to come in either. It's a step forward.

"You don't belong here anymore," she says.

"You never stop belonging to Underguater."

You walk into the small room. A smeared stove attempts to warm up some old pots filled with food. The bathroom is as small as those in the space station. It's open, dirty, and lacks tiles. Next to the window, she gazes into the sea. You get closer. What she is gazing upon is not the interior lake of Havana. It's the real ocean that expands in front of the city like a blue desert.

"The neighborhood is the same as when I left," you say

more to break the ice than to start conversation. "You are too."

"In Underguater nothing changes. Ever. But you have changed. You look more... Russian."

"Have you heard anything from him?"

"Who? Ricardo Miguel...? I don't understand why you ask me about him. After you went up there, he left for the Malayan-Korean-Japanese complex. You must know more about him than I do."

"He doesn't write?"

"Neither do you."

"He doesn't send anything for the boy either?"

"Did you ever send anything? My son is not any of your business. Yours or his."

"I have to know. Even he should know too."

"No."

"No, what?"

"Just no. It's easy to go to orbit with the Russians or to Asia with the non-Catholic corporations. Let time go by and come back to ask: Is your son mine or his? Like that makes a difference. Like that's going to pay for all I've been through, alone, with a child in the middle of this nest of aseres. I had to go through plenty of sacrifices to feed him, educate him, make sure he goes beyond the limited horizon of everyone around here. And now that he's grown up, now that he did not become an asere or a hacker, now that he has a decent job in the Ifá Navy... You land in Havana just to ask if he's yours! What if I tell you he is? You're going to worry about him now? You're going to take him to live in a luxurious orbital station with the Russians...? And if I tell you he is Ricardo Miguel's, what will you do? You will go to the sunken plaza at the Cathedral, go to the space station, board a rocket, and we will never see you again. Will you have the courage to find Ricardo Miguel with one of the espionage satellites over Asia? Would you have the courage to tell him that my son is also his? No. I won't say anything to either of you. My son is not from any of you two. He is mine and that's it."

"But one of us is the father."

"Like Ricardo Miguel would say: The mathematical probability that either of you is the father is one over two. Of course one of you is the father. But knowing it doesn't change anything for him."

You know very well that she won't tell you anything. That she doesn't care that the Russians don't treat orbital immigrants as equals. That the luxury and low gravity come at a price. She doesn't care that Ricardo Miguel is little more than a slave programming zeros and ones in a bunker in Pyongyang. In her eyes there is only Underguater. The troubles she's had to go through to raise a son in the middle of a warzone. Her and that ocean she had always wanted to cross. Neither you nor Ricardo Miguel ever wanted to get out of here. You wanted to be the toughest asere in Downtown Havana. Ricardo Miguel, the best hacker. Your horizons never reached that far. But there was her.

That girl who spoke of the tomb of Che in Autonomous Santa Clara. Of the special troops that held honor guards with their black uniforms. Of the devoted who arrived there walking all the way from Autonomous Santiago following the Invasion Route. The sacred path of Guevara. She also spoke of the sanctuary at La Higuera, in Bolivia, where there was the Firing Squad Chapel. The place where the Holy Insurgent had died. She spoke of the towers at the New Vatican in Dublin, of the battleships of the desert that guarded the oil wells in Saudi Israel. Of the Kremlin, in Old Russia, of the corporate islands in the oceans of China. Of the Russian space stations that patrolled everything from the sky.

And she filled their heads with dreams. And the horizon at the edge of the ocean grew and grew. And you two had no choice but to love her. And the baby arrived. And the realization that you both had loved her in a sick and selfish way. Insufficient to share her. And you fought. And you both felt ashamed of fighting in front of her. Of endangering the life of the child out of pure and simple selfishness. And you left. And he left. But she had to stay.

Nobody gives a working contract in the corporate complexes to a woman with a small child. No guerrilla community would accept a member with a baby in her arms. She had to stay. And keep gazing into the horizon, more with the heart than with the eyes.

You know she will never tell you. You assume Ricardo Miguel has tried in vain too. That is why he will never come back. But you have to know. You don't want to keep playing the Russian lapdog. You don't want to keep looking down at Havana. You care about this city, half collapsing, you care about its dirty waters that run through the sunken streets, you even care about the FULHA helicopters that fly over the buildings, like bad omen birds. And, above everything else, you want to look into the eyes of that young boy who calls the woman you once loved "mother." To know if his eyes are yours or his. No matter the consequences. You just have to know.

You look at the clock. It's late, you have waited long enough. The boy will soon come back home. She doesn't have to say anything. You will know just by looking at him.

There are footsteps on the stairs. You remember you never closed the door. It was a clever maneuver to see him as soon as he came upstairs.

Several people appear on the threshold. There are three of the boys with whom you fought downstairs. They come with two other guys. Tall, strong, and with bulletproof vests. Professional aseres. Possibly uncles or father of the one you killed. Or of the one whose arm you broke. This neighborhood will never change. And for the first time in many years you feel happy. You are at home. You can take care of this before the boy gets back.

"Come and show us how tough you are now!" one of the boys says. "Try to break his arm, come on."

"Whose, his?" you point at one of the aseres as you walk toward the door.

One of them takes out a gun. It is a CZ. Your instructors trained you to call it Česká Zbrojovka. But in Havana it has always been called CZ and you are not in orbit anymore.

You jump on top of the asere before he even draws it. You two wrestle. He tries to take his gun. You apply a chokehold and you use him as a shield. The shot from the CZ lands in the vest of the asere. You break the neck of your hostage and you take his gun.

You shoot the Makarov before the CZ. A clean shot to the forehead. One of the boys jumps over you and makes you lower your gun. You feel the cold of the steel on your ribs. You let go of the gun, you hit the neck of the boy. You move between the other two. Gravity upsets you and the stab hurts. You hit them with anger. You break their bones, fracture their necks. You kill them in a simple yet poorly efficient manner. Your Russian instructors of martial arts would reprehend you if they saw you. But they are not here. Gravity makes you dizzy, you hit the ground.

"You're old. Too many years of the good life have made you slow," she says bending down over you.

You feel her hands trying to heal the wound. You also feel the blood flowing.

"You should have never come back."

You hear footsteps on the stairs. It must be him. It's almost certain that it is him.

You don't have the strength to turn your head. You make one last effort. You look, but everything is dark. One last whirl of dizziness makes you feel like a Proton-II knocked out of orbit.

"Mom, what happened! Are you okay?"

You get to hear it. But you can't see anything anymore. Around you everything is turning blurrier and blurrier.

(i) Balseros: slang term used for Cubans who cross the Gulf of Mexico in a raft or boat to get to Cuba from the US.

(ii) Abakuas: member of Afro-Cuban religious fraternity.

(iii) Santeros: practitioners of Santeria, an Afro-Cuban religion that syncretizes Yoruba religion with Roman Catholicism.

(iv) Babalawo: a high priest of Ifá in the Yoruba religion.

Sunflower Fields Forever

Story by Orlando Luis Pardo Lazo

Translated by Alison Macomber

1.

They read rather decadent things: Little novels of characters who committed suicide just before the authors who wrote them, second-hand editions as useful as recycled paper, banned books, unpublished pamphlets, raw gems, and etceteras of this style. Of course, reading decadent things made them think that they lived in "an absurd era, of little or no action, as often happens after great revolutions or little catastrophes." A quote that they both liked very much and that could have come from *Silvia*, by Gerard de Nerval (Orlando's favorite), or from *Orlando*, by Virginia Woolf (Silvia's favorite). In any case, they loved to be the protagonists of such beautiful and sad desperation. Thus, they were now waiting for the first opportunity to act.

Every night, very late, Orlando called her to say: "Silvia, nothing happens, but it hurts me," she in silence. Every night, by telephone, Orlando would repeat: "Silvia, I am not me, but you won't be you again," she in silence. Until, every night, Orlando assaulted her by provoking her: "Silvia, it is useless to hope for love to come: I wish I never knew you," she in silence, without paying enough attention to his pathetics.

"Fear kills you, Orlando," said Silvia's calm voice.

And then he felt rage. A resentment that drilled everything inside: Spiked worms in his brain, screaming in a schizo chorus of terrible tuning. Orlando shook with a desire to kill her, from behind, without warning. The desire to tear that magnificent skull into a thousand and one pieces with the phone. The pleasure of spitting an obscenity precisely at his love: "Silvia, die!" for example, and hang up the phone without giving her a chance to react. And just like that Orlando did it, angry to the point of imbecility: "Silvia, die!" and hung up without giving her a chance to react.

For two or three minutes he closed his eyes and breathed considerably better. Suddenly he felt like the most desolate and sincere being in the universe. For two or three minutes Orlando read, tattooed on his chest, the acronym of that crazy word: *l.i.b.e.r.t.a.d.* At last he was free from Silvia, and Silvia was free from him. Without decadent readings or free radicals in their neurons: Beyond wreckage and rescue, almost beyond the stagnation and the revolution. Silvia was finally free from Orlando, and Orlando was also free from her.

Until a cold paralyzed his lungs and stomach, and twisted it to the point of panic and pain. An almost physical mental ulcer. A vomit that pushed his teeth out for being so violent and empty. Then Orlando opened his eyes maddeningly and picked up the phone, capturing all of the helplessness of Lawton, his neighborhood. Panicking, he dialed her number in Guanabacoa, flying over the six keystrokes that separated him from Silvia like a madman.

And when Silvia's voice answered, Orlando couldn't even say *Silvia*. Nor save me. Nor anything else. He could only swallow a dead paste, without saliva, before throwing up a sort of silent cry—his childish way of apologizing: "Forgive me, Silvia," she in silence. "Forgive me, Silvia, I didn't want it to be that way," she in silence. "Forgive me, Silvia, I did not want it to be that way, or any other way either," she in silence, already ready to be God and resurrect Orlando with her mercy: The two touching themselves until they were nauseous on the over-voltage of that state-owned telephone line.

All. All the wee hours. In all the wee hours of Lawton and Guanabacoa it happened like this. A miniature tragedy which ended with whimpers and laughter and squeals of delight. All, all, all the wee hours. They wanted to float in the foam of a boring age, and such a delirium seemed entertainingly genial. They wanted to sink in the zero years of the 2000's. And they suspected an end of something and a beginning of a nothing that, from reading to reading, Orlando and Silvia felt that Silvia and Orlando were about to protagonize.

2.

For Orlando, sitting in the park of Street B was the cruelest way to experience horror. They always went there in Lawton, between flamboyants and sparrows bitten by the national sun. There was an area full of holes built for shelter during times of peace, anti-aircraft pools flooded by decades of rain and fermentation. A block ravaged by barbaric neighbors fighting against their benches, lanterns, and paths. Over the meandering rivers of sewer witchcraft. Over their seesaws and swings with rust and termites. Over the pines stunted by the excessive Cuban light. Over Silvia just arriving by bus from Guanabacoa; her gaze unfocused because of the limitlessness of Lawton.

For Silvia, sitting in Park B was the friendliest way to experience horror, feeling less alone hugging him: Being almost inside of Orlando. And there they headed, noon after noon. To do nothing. To look at each other. To kill the time and the perennial nervous breakdown in which they survived. To tremble and to pass the pages. To read little volumes of paper as deteriorated as the landscape, or wasteland. To feel lost in the readings, unsung heroes that no suicidal writer would write about. They were letting the official names of the years pass by. Without history and time, Orlando and Silvia without names, without past or future: Creatures of a pure, over-saturated present, gasping the air of the barred city. And nothing seemed more exciting than this day-to-day progression without rules or consequences, this cluster of stories bought in bulk from the moths and tedium of a state library.

From Street B, they let the buses, stinking like tractor trailers and liverwort, pass by Porvenir Avenue. From there they counted, as if they were at a lookout on ground level, the drunks without a homeland whose livers hadn't murdered them yet. From there Silvia and Orlando mutually admired—almost grateful to God, or to the chronic lack of God—having that boring bench to read and entertainingly love each other on and, hopefully, from month to month and from millennium to millennium, privately resist the cruel and friendly experience of such a public horror.

3.

They drove between cars, dodging honks and squealing brakes, mocking traffic lights hanging by their necks, without believing in any message or signal. They had decided that there had been a lesson sufficient enough. For this reason they hated this lovely city: Because of its style of a permanent classroom, of cloistered uniformity, of a little disciplinary school impossible to ignore or transform. They waited for the right moment for each other, before emitting a howl and pouncing, like cunning beasts, on what, who, or for why they couldn't yet say.

For the moment they drove blindly on his motorbike, a Júpiter with cannibalized pieces of a Harley Davidson. On the Júpiter-Davidson they were merged into a single body, Orlando and Silvia alternatively sticking their nails into each other, depending on who was driving, penetrated on the promise of making themselves free before finally making love: The promise of waiting so as to not feel guilty beneath the shapeless inertia of repetition. For the moment they drove at night, discussing the sights that caught their attention at that time, when they seemed most likely invented, from neighborhood to neighborhood, the barbarity of a map more theatrical than gloomy: An open book abandoned even by its anonymous author.

"Silvia, the lover of Virginia Woolf, jumped off of that roof," was said on Ñ St. and 23rd. "Orlando, in this encampment the Cuban Nazi Party was founded," was said on San Lázaro and Lealtad streets. "Silvia, this curved building is a sickle and its tower would be a hammer," was said on Línea and L. "Orlando, buried under those bronze shoes is the broken kneecap of Gerard de Nerval," was said on the Avenue of the Presidents and Malecón.

Driving together cheered them up, and chased away the tedium of driving together. Havana was filled with foolish and breathable images, and it seemed fun and rebellious to retell everything again just for them, from zero and even less, without ever stopping for any scenery, and without remembering the next night which detail was false and which was true.

"Silvia, Orlando, Virginia Woolf's best character, died in this asylum," was said on Dolores and Acosta. "Orlando, in the ruins of this restaurant the atomic reactor of Jaraguá still operates in secret," was said on Infanta and P. "Silvia, there is a night of the world when the bay tunnel connects two times with the same shore," was said on Prado and La Punta. "Orlando, in this church there is a chalice with Silvia's blood that does not clot, Gerard de Nerval's worst character," was said on Novena and 84th.

They drove, taking turns steering, until they were tired, until they were leaning over the exhausted gas tank. Then, they dropped the motorbike in the first State parking lot they could find, took a taxi, paid in dollars, and in twenty minutes each one was back in their rooms: Lying upon the beds they fell onto, the two already ready for the telephone, with that terrible and tender offensive ritual, crying, forgiveness, and pleasure through a cable.

This happened during all the wee hours. All the wee hours. All of them. In Guanabacoa and in Lawton and all over the world: They resisted or pretended to resist. Until a minimal variation was sufficient enough for Orlando and Silvia to unravel this story that was sewn only for them to be its protagonists.

4.

In the liquid noon of Park B, Silvia appeared with a revolver. "This is from my grandfather," she said. "Look at the date on the handle: 1910." Orlando was motivated: "The year of the murderer comet. In 1910 the twentieth century should have disappeared by its own will."

Silvia pulled him towards her on the bench. She put Orlando's head on her lap and leaned forward to cover his head from the zenithal sun. Orlando closed his eyes. The glare was too much, and went through the strands of Silvia's hair like a silk palm tree or a crystal pyramid. The same heat burned for the entire year. Reality evaporated for them, and it made them angry to exist like this, humid and humiliated, without the illusion of those Novembers described in any random open or closed book.

Orlando asked for the revolver. He licked it. The revolver tasted like ferrous hemoglobin, like a dried salty residue of iodine, even though it was kept far from the sea. He tangentially blew into that century-old canon, improvising the playing motions of a funeral flute: "It feels like this is carved from the tibia of a whore or from the femur of a man who has been shot," he said without opening his eyes. The sound remitted the lethal tunes of a wedding march. This wild whistle awakened something in Silvia, and when the death relic was returned to her, he heard her make a decision: "It's now or now, Orlando, we can't be so mediocre and lose this opportunity."

And, without feeling the need to draw back his eyelids, Orlando knew she smiled beautifully bent over him: Her mouth open like a cave, like the cracked crater from a spring. It was very easy for Orlando to feel Silvia's joy because, from where he was, he could almost chew the warm steam of her laughter. Silvia's breath was made of fruits nonexistent in this fierce climate: Grapes, pears, apples, and those rare almonds without shells. Orlando pretended to be a wine taster and in an inaudible voice he spoke to the world, to all, in a cry of war for his love: "We will do it because today Silvia tastes like a murderer comet, a frustrated harvest from 1910."

5.

So they went to the ground mines of Guanabacoa. They packed a large backpack where the revolver was hidden, floating like a kidnapped baby in a placenta of bullets: A hundred, a thousand, a hundred-thousand projectiles of light caliber. On one side of the cemetery they advanced toward the national freeway, an endless eight-way strip. "The 8 is an infinity symbol, but it's standing up," Orlando heard Silvia shout from the back seat. "And also a closed, double S, without claustrophobia but without liberty," she continued.

Night was falling, and they left behind the rabid divisions of martyred and vulgar names. They passed dairy farms, foundries, high-voltage towers and others for fuel extraction, and also desperate fields of flowers for sale: Most of them were sunflowers, heads twitching like fists at that time of day. Finally, the Júpiter-Davidson's motor stopped at the decayed mouth of the quarries, with the moon bouncing between the cliffs until falling into the silver lagoon. From afar, the fields of sunflowers looked like a stationary parade that the next morning someone would decapitate. Then Orlando doubted: "Do we do it now, Silvia?" and she replied by taking off her clothes right there, straddling the lukewarm fuel tank.

Orlando was still clutching the handlebars when Silvia pointed the revolver at his neck. Silvia put the first ten or ten thousand bullets in the drum, and loaded the gun with a click-clack. Then she ordered him to undress too. After this, for her, a mocking English phrase was enough to begin the scene that will, in turn, start rolling for the rest of the film: "Run for your life," laughed Silvia, and she began shooting.

Orlando ran naked like a moon sliver. He fled for his life, but without fear, as had been agreed upon, feeling the pecking whirrs around him: Nocturnal sparrows diving fatally. Underneath his feet, the sharp quartz stabbed him to the bone with each spin, and the drops of blood cooled that beautiful, almost-criminal scene: A red fluid flowed from Orlando becoming frost from the coldness of his sweat.

Many minutes of fleeing passed. A half hour, or an hour and a half maybe. He finally fell, exhausted. Breathing thanks to the sibilants, his pores were little tracheotomies straight to his lungs. Silvia had shot a little less than two thousand bullets, like the year, and now their backpack seemed empty after that rehearsal of an anti-personal mine war. Orlando panted, his sternum wanting to crack, and his asthma competing with the wind's blades that sharpened the cliffs, shaving the quartz into a diamond. *Shine on you Cuban diamond.*

He crawled a few feet to the edge of the lagoon. He looked up. He saw a double metal moon. And then he drank twice. The water, or the light, was brackish. He felt nauseous, but he swallowed that moldy fluid, oily and pure, seminal more than sidereal. And then he was completely introduced into that solid sea, still gripping a stone shaped in the form of a handle. Then he felt Silvia's silhouette, giving him her hand while warning Orlando: "Come, at night the water is more treacherous than the rest of reality."

He went outward and began to kiss all of her skin, stopping first at her armpits and after at her naval doormat: The shaggy mane that tattooed her pelvis. They hugged trembling, in a half fever, half chill. They cynically manipulated their genitals under the celibate heaven of Cuba, but neither intended to make love. Not yet that night. The two still lacked enough words for such an act: A tragic luxury and a release. Both of them still felt plenty of panic. So they remained there, onanist-angelical virgins, until shortly before dawn when the whole cosmos looked mauve and then orange, and then yellow and then white, and then colorless and then blue: Cyan-aqua necrotic stripes, where neither day nor night could completely erase what was among them.

The idea was to recover and then do the opposite in broad daylight: Silvia practiced her best style of flight, her naked body under the sun's rays, while Orlando pointed the remaining bullets, ready to miss. But as dawn was getting higher and higher, a hysterical howling of sirens and speakers came from the other side of the cliffs. The siege had begun, or perhaps, already, the assault.

Silvia and Orlando got dressed before peering over the cliff to view the ostentatious police convoy, drawing cross-country esses between the rows of sunflowers, cutting the throats of their oily heads, scraping a blurred Van-Gogh that, from the height from which they were entrenched, seemed better than any painting or painter. The shootings in the wee hours had probably given their game away: Orlando said something like ("This is a land without weapons") and Silvia nodded with a yawn that he changed into a kiss, just when her lips were at the maximum point of tension ("This is a country without a soul," she whispered). Orlando thought that, surely, the vapor of Silvia's mouth was more eternal than the very word "Silvia" that defined it.

They held hands. Paradoxically, their breathing slowed down, as did their pulse and the nervousness in which they survived. And they decided in unison, with a glance, without the need to see each other again, their eyes lost in the horizon, from where the authority was already urging them to surrender without escape and without resistance.

It was the time without time, that of Orlando and Silvia, that of Silvia and Orlando: In any order of anarchy and despair. Neither wanted to erase the acronyms that stood for freedom from each other: *l.i.b.e.r.t.a.d.*: A puzzle they would never regret, only sure of this under the threat of dawn. Besides, it had been so long since they were hoping for a gap like this, that it was already pointless to forget it or think it again. Now, a first gesture of reaction was enough. An act, an expression, a blow: After living within the words of so much decadent culture, the verb "to act" was now the only verb that was worthwhile for them to spell.

6.

They fled on his motorcycle through the rear gutters, through that archipelago of florid and bland villages that eventually lead to Tarará. And from there, straight through Vía Blanca, toward Matanzas or to the posthumous bridge of Bacunayagua—the altar of local suicides—whether or not they wrote books where the characters killed themselves a little before or after the author who wrote them.

Orlando drove furiously, throwing up asphalt at top speed, while Silvia encouraged him, wedged between his kidneys and his vertebrae, sitting open like scissors on the back seat. They were a little queasy, but they went through the stampede with a euphoric calmness. They fled: Fugitives capable of any action. And this vital energy breathed the vertigo of a free fall into them. At last, it was they who were making things happen. Or at least they were refusing to let them happen indolently. So, at any moment, they couldn't keep quiet, tripping over plans in unison that neither Orlando nor Silvia comprehended very well, as the 200 or 2,000 km/hr gusts of wind kidnapped their voices.

The motor reverberated like the remaining reality: Its remains of unreality. One thing they both understood that made them laugh a lot, the crazy laughter that escapes from a State ambulance: From now on he would always be Orlando Woolf ("A proud wolf in honor of Virginia," he said), and she would always be Silvia de Nerval ("A volatile vision of Gerard's V's," she said). Renaming themselves seemed to be the best clinical symptom of the eight, infinite acronyms of the word: *l.i.b.e.r.t.a.d.*

And it was very strange. The landscape did not advance. Palms, carobs, kapoks, and flamboyants splashed with primary colors. Cows and horses, plows and tractors, old people of centuries and children of weeks, women and soldiers. The lines of the pavement homogenized the sketches of the journey. Everything was flying before their eyes, but the landscape didn't seem to advance. Orlando Woolf and Silvia de Nerval revolved in a bubble of kinetic exception, in a freeze-frame of any local road-movie: A very strange inertia that, to them, seemed like a habitual ancestral miracle.

The Júpiter-Davidson roared like a dragon's throat. It spat sparks through the four ports of the exhaust pipe, dragging a string of murky smoke more turbo than turbid. A racing comet on concrete. The White Road looked unrecognizable that morning. Orlando Woolf felt Silvia de Nerval's lips on his neck, where just hours before she had nailed the deadly 1910 canon: "Cuba is so slow," he heard her complain: "Love, can you just speed up?" And he loudly explained that the pistons were already about to melt into national plasma. Then they turned the corner of North Santa Cruz and, even though they saw nothing, they both felt a dry blow that shattered the headlights and the lights into shards that covered them in a paste or fine powder.

They instinctively looked back, without stopping. And

they saw a kind of blue puppet, zigzagging between the eight lanes; red ink jets were launched from its extremities, drawing an illegible graffiti on the road. "Did we kill a cop?" Orlando Woolf hesitated after such an obvious image. And Silvia de Nerval waited several seconds or kilometers before she responded: "Hopefully we did."

It made no sense to stop at the scene, and even less for an accident. They were involved and the price of being free was still the same. The rubber of the tires became viscous and, from the crash, they drove without being sure if they retreated forward or if they continued in reverse. In fact, Orlando Woolf now scratched her back, and Silvia de Nerval guided the helm over the fresh footprints of the bike that, without a doubt, were those of their own Júpiter-Davidson a few minutes or kilometers back: The static passage gave them the impression that they were just turning back on their own breaks. They moved in fast-forward upwind, but downwind in *rewind*.

So they crossed the railroad lines and recognized the outlines of the rickety pines against the light and the flamboyants without birds, cut above the same grass without neighbors or banks or streetlights or paths: An infected slew of infantile diversion machines as threatening as prehistoric dinosaurs. Again, it was the provincial park of Street B, just a couple of blocks from Porvenir Avenue.

Silvia de Nerval didn't stop. Nor did she even flinch. Nor did she warn Orlando Woolf about it, although he already knew about it, and he, in turn, fought against his astonishment that Silvia didn't notice it, shaking at the steering wheel, traversing a shortcut to the staircase of the State convent. No other explanation was necessary: The naught neighborhood of Lawton reappeared the more they moved away from it. Then Silvia de Nerval tangentially crossed the ballpark, and at once they regained, in wide angle, the vision of those fields of flowers for sale that swarmed in the outskirts of Guanabacoa: Desperate sunflowers in their majority, still with the drooling scars of the police assault from which they thought or sought to be fleeing.

A few more meters, and the Júpiter-Davidson was back at the decayed mouth of the quarries, with the moon bouncing between the cliffs until falling into the silver lagoon. Suddenly, they sensed that the whole escape was only an illusion, because the zero time of the year 2000 returned to them the four, very fulminate acronyms of the century: *c.u.b.a.* everywhere, *c.u.b.a.* for all of the ages, c.u.b.a. as gratuitous and obligatory freedom, c.u.b.a. as ubiquitous *cu*biquity, *c.u.b.a.* as scaffold.

In fact, they were surrounded by the authorities again and so it was impossible to distinguish. Nor resist, nor escape, nor nothing. It was a cosmic, closed cycle. But Big-Boring more than Big-Bang. Orlando and Silvia aborted their anxious desires to be protagonists, like their last-minute surnames. Or precisely the opposite: Each were thankful to be followed and surrounded because Silvia and Orlando could now perform their birth of death, or maybe their pact of life. An act not as gloomy as it was theatrical. The debacle of returning to themselves seemed to be the shortest way to finally be another.

7.

The quarries shimmered. The patriotic quartz crackled furiously in their pupils. From the moon's milky hole, a rabbit skull grimaced obscenely, despite the rising sun. They felt so alien and so part of it all... So ambiguous, so distant, so final and so close, that this had to be the end...

They settled on the Júpiter-Davidson, the mechanical horse collage with pieces in Cyrillic and English. Orlando was once again at the steering wheel. He accelerated. They smelled the reheated gasoline at dawn, with its most intimate, home-distilled alcohols. He removed the hand brake and Silvia stood on tiptoe on the four wind pipes of the tail-pipe. The bike reared up, still standing, two-footed doing acrobatic stunts on the rear tire. And, without even agreeing, Orlando and Silvia hurled a dry howl that evaporated the remaining morning dew. Howl. Aullido. Howllido.

They jumped. Only then they remembered that, despite remembering it well, they still weren't dressed. The bike began to rise in a crazy parabola above the cliff and, once in the air, they discovered that they were as naked as they were during the previous wee hours. The military deployment that almost caught them remained below. More than reading it, this was an unread self-dissolving scene, a pose literally taken from a film: Plagiarism of two thousand or so cheap movies, where the script of the final scene jumps over the barrier of verisimilitude. Orlando and Silvia knew very well that it was all just a show. Silvia and Orlando knew very well that, in that instant, precisely because of this, they manipulated the innermost threads of reality.

They heard the fanfare of the speakers and the hysteria of the sirens. From below their pursuers seemed to be a toy army. Above the horizon in the form of a noose, they craved the clouds to be loaded with water and electricity: Delocalized waves in an insoluble, unfathomable equation. The silver lagoon was nothing more than "An uncirculated currency of 1910," he said: "The spit of an exiled god put in a comet," he said, "the surface of a mirror with nothing to reflect."

At some point Silvia stopped screaming in the air and said: "I see nothing from back here." Orlando immediately consoled her: "There isn't much to see." With a jovial tone: "Down there it just seems like quarries of dead quartz and fields of sunflowers that are about to be executed." In return, she emitted a brief "hopefully," compressed almost into one syllable, and then they both laughed, floating in the peak of the parabola, the two weightless but already at the point of regaining the mass lost after their impulse.

Orlando felt that Silvia pushed with her best strength. Her breasts drilled his lungs and came out on both sides of his sternum. Silvia threatened him again through his back: She had him at gunpoint or was devouring from behind. Orlando felt Silvia's savage hands, placed as opaque lenses under his eyelids, putting her fingers in roots, scraping off his retina. Now he could not even see, perhaps because he didn't care about anything at all. Not seeing is the best way to stare. Gram by gram, the bike regained its gravity, and descended with avidity to make itself fragments against a vocabulary of heavy words, outfashioned, compressed to a single syllable, or to the whole of an official vocubalario.

And there, the sleepless magic of waiting months or millennia to make love consumed itself. That mortal somersault was the climax of an unfree fall from which they wanted or believed they could flee. That was the only option that, the two blind over the ravine, could finally choose to resist and escape: "Choose, love," he said: "Dead quartz quarries or fields of sunflowers soon to be executed?" Even though she, for all answers, only penetrated him a little more, until overflowing him inside and filling both bodies with Silvia, after that dizzying and voracious selection: "Of course, sunflower fields forever," she calmly pronounced. "Even though the fear kills you, Orlando, eternity is still to be exercised."

8.

The following midnight, after another long and narrow day's journey of reading rather decadent things, they were consequently convinced that they lived in "an absurd era, of little or no action, as often happens after great revolutions or little catastrophes,"—a quote that they both liked very much and that could have come from Silvia, by Gerard de Nerval (Orlando's favorite), or from Orlando, by Virginia Woolf (Silvia's favorite)—he picked up the phone and desperately flew over her six keystrokes. As usual, through the tone of their bundled voices, it was evident that their unwoven story was only now about to begin.

Dis Tortue, Dors-Tu Nue?

Story by Lia Villares

Translated by Juan O. Tamayo

Fog in the mornings, hunger for clarity,
coffee and bread with sour plum jam.
Numbness of soul in placid neighborhoods.
Lives ticking on as if.
—Adrienne Rich

B gets up and goes to the shower. Doesn't close doors or draw curtains. The water runs vaporously, terrifyingly. Bends to open the blinds, the gown open.

"Dis-moi, what is the best?"

"The best and the worst, like the Bukowski poem?"

"For him, it was the whores, the beer. The worst: The work, the police stations, the terminals."

"Let's see, the best is to bathe together. And your mother's rice pudding."

"For me, the best is the light. Your skin, the hues, what I can't manage to see, what I see too much of. Before and after, the nights at the Cinemateque, with Helmut Kautner. The photography course only-for-aficionados. The watery and hot cappuccinos on the little table beneath the fly trap: Electric trap for bugs, shaking us with each capture, zapping sound included. Without changing places, reading the tired, almost-never-happy faces of the regulars. We're dying with disgust. More. The couples stopped by the window pane, faces of hand-holders looking for a place, some empty table for two. The estrangement always evoked by the discredit or that childish surprise over everything that at some point was drawn on its own face. Youthful exhibitors of daily stupidity, an expanded emptiness. The crazy guy with his Walkman moving his head, or paying attention in the dark hall to the fleeting hand that slides along the peeled walls of the stairways of Wong Kar-Wai. The waitresses vomiting their boredom into cups. A vomit of sorrow. Of lack of desire and insignificance."

"And what else?"

"The alcohol burner and the saltpeter, one guitar-playing friend used to say. Linen clothes, sans doute. To read Bukowski on the toilet. To write dirty poems."

"Bob Dylan in halves: Midnight and half a bottle of whisky for two."

"Tim Burton poems in the Inbox."

"The best, j'insiste, does not include me?"

"Let me see... What's missing are new books, to hibernate under the blankets, the slippers from Quito..."

"Count Basie. Your bedroom at three in the afternoon, if it was possible to isolate it from the telephone-streets-buses."

"Black tea, chocolate with cinnamon. Milord at the accordion, Edith on the speakers."

"Now you're starting to include me."

After and before on the night buses, fuller than the moon and the bellies. The windows open, stained with collective sweat. To linger, watching a fat woman leaning on a grey, dirty wall. A tiny dress the color of skin, the bare skin coming out of the scanty, tight silk. The girl(s) of thirteen, the downy hair behind the neck, the back, the bony shoulders. Straps fallen from a blouse that holds in the hint of all-too noticeable areolas. (Just looking at her you get goose bumps. When a seat is free you take it, and fast, to be direct: Come, don't you want to sit on me? And she does not hesitate: She leans back, her lightness taking your breath away.) The loose hairs the color of chamomile, or our braided knots. Both of our hairs messing up with the wind on our faces at the speed of the night. Her glances, lost inside the walls that remained, from rubble to rubble, searching for some color that does not exist, for some hue alive in appearance.

More or less, never so much, mix a bit of that with the rest as though it were just the preparation of home-made rice pudding, something exclusive, or nothing.

When you are here the contagion is unavoidable. The sensible, irrational. The order, chaos. A scary clarity, without a doubt. Although sometimes the city is also part of the home, and of the thing itself. I dress in the most light-colored clothes to go out on the street. It's noon and it's hot, 89 degrees. Crushing, crazy for February. The days that begin with those kinds of signs presage a touch of the unusual, but nothing more happens.

I arrive again. I try to call B: The-cell-that-you-are-calling-is-turned-off-or-outside-the-coverage-area. I use the time to check the Inbox. The milk and the cheese and the bread and the tomato mix in my mouth. I listen to Bebel Gilberto, tanto tempo, the song says. I swallow slowly. The monitor reflects the picture window, with all the wires branching out from the electrical poles. It is almost night again. I go back to the street.

We left Strawberry and Chocolate after more than five beers a piece —B later said at least ten— to get more money and finish up in the first slummy hovel on our way.

On the second block, from inside a car, a bald head sticks out and shouts at us. I vaguely recognize an old friend from secondary school. He is much fatter and I see that he's the one driving. Inside are two other guys, strangers.

We're all inside quickly, windows up, passing the joint amid the smoke and the guitar that one of the guys holds. At the top of the lungs, the last hit by *Gente D'Zona*.

Look at her, look how she sweats, how she strips, she doesn't know, that my tuba broke...

The lyrics are a mystery. We start to catch the enthusiasm, slowly. B looks at me and I don't see a desperate expression, I don't see anything, her reddish eyes go through me and out through the tinted glass, I don't want to take care of her. I can't see.

All ages had been boring for B from the beginning, from her mute knowledge of a deserted city, more dead each day.

Always in a hurry to sleep again, although even awake it could be said that she slept. Sleep again to lose everything. More nothingness. Emptiness. More nothing.

Between my feet the whiskers, the slow tail, the wet nose. My cat is hungry. Sometimes for love more than for food. I get cold. I pick him up, he weighs a bit, I leave him on the rug. I sit on the floor. I am hungry also.

Anamnesia... Why didn't you name him Anaximandro, if you wanted something very unusual?

B sleeps.

We got off at a *Rapido* snackbar in Vedado. The crazy one with the guitar, who was also the one now driving, shouts to everyone from the door that the music had arrived at the cemetery.

The place is full, despite the late hour. I want more beer, I shout also. We take over the first table and we number about six. I ask B if she's well, if she wants to go to the bathroom. Everyone looks at us like intruders, but they quickly return to their cans. One goes to the bar to ask for beers and demand with screams that they shut off the shrill music on the stereo, to warm up the place.

I go with B. The door to the bathroom doesn't close, and has a big hole in the middle where the lock should be. There are three men ahead who look like they work in the place. I ask them to let us go in. They let us pass in between guffaws and say something about remuneration, paying them for guarding the door. They look alternately at us and the group, which has taken over a double table, the guy with the guitar has just jumped on a table and to my surprise sings an old ballad from Sancti Spiritus' troubadours. His voice is more powerful than three stereos together.

Herminia those phrases that you spilled, they should not be spilled by women.

I tell B to go in and I stay outside guarding. The bald guy comes and brings me a beer and puts two lollypops in my shirt pocket. Strawberry, he says, and leaves again. B opens the door, comes out putting her hair up with a clip, and the gesture slows down, repeats. On her face the lack of expression becomes even more tranquil.

Around the table a new group of five or six women, lured from outside by the music, now sway and sing in a chorus for the one with the guitar. The voltage of their singing keeps rising, toward the roof, and someone comes to ask that we lower the volume. Everyone is having fun, he says and looks like that means him too, but there are neighbors upstairs who could call the police because of the racket.

No one pays any mind. Far from dropping, the voices rise. My beer is finished and I grab the bottle of Legendario rum that's near me. To get used to the guys, these guys, is not so difficult, after all, and I take a deep swig. I pass the bottle to B, who turns it down without looking at me, happy yet removed.

There were days of not going out, of going nowhere, to have no hunger or die from the hunger pangs... days to step on ants, gather leaves, wash our faces and hands in the sour-sweet-salty water of a fountain, throw rice to the most daring birds... days to not-do, nothing, talk to no one, sleep all hours, stay under the shower, under the falling happiness, to land on both feet... days for nothing-at-all.

Days in which it was not possible to wake up, to write letters, comb one's hair or listen, nothing, anything, cockroaches under the lumber, dust falling on the books, doves crashing into window panes. Days of mosquito netting.

There were days for not-needing, for not putting on faces, of not-having-to-say, nothing, no salutations or farewells to be left on a paper-on-the-table. Days to break down, lose things, find rocks. Days to grow tired before-it-is-time, to grow grouchy-in-vain, answer no doors nor calls nor the pen, nor desire. Days for not even. Days to go backward, walk more, run up the hill.

On the street, upanddown, we were riding again in the runaway Nissan. I saw that B was beginning to feel sick. I saw how bad she was. More than pale, pasty, chilled.

The bald guy was driving out of control. I shouted to him, above the very loud CD player, to stop so B could throw up. I opened the door and bent her head down by the neck. We were again starting to be in the least expected place. Very difficult situations. It was too much alcohol for B, who got dizzy on two beers. To preserve a minimum of clarity in the face of apparent chaos, a minimum level of organization. That had been my slogan after more than a couple of memorable embarrassments in memorably public places, when large quantities of alcohol still made me throw up.

B looks fragile, not now, she always gave the impression of something brittle, far behind her bottomless eyes there was the weakness of a rag doll, of a plant that wants to be abandoned. Protection, company, words with a meaning too strange and not at all desirable. If she needed anything it would be to remain alone, standing, awake, alive. Absorbed in that thought I believed, I think I believed, that I heard the sound of an oriental, sensual, flute, two long notes separated by B's strange breathing, worrying, broken, nervous. Distant.

She was no longer at my side, I got out of the car as fast as I could, one hand grabbed me hard on the shoulder and, before I knew it, another pulled me from behind and held my face under the nose for all the time in the world, all the time of a human life.

B braids and unbraids her hair in a hypnotic do-undo. The man's shirt is smudged with dried tooth paste. Crayolas strewn on the bed.

To reach the absurd, in between death and the routine reserved for a dilapidated city, it is necessary to kill all sensibility. Sensibility is hope.

B writes with a green Crayola on the wall, above the bed.

She throws the book that she's copying from on the floor, and lies down, face down. The room is in the red semi-darkness of a small lamp. To persist in the idea of an absolute sadness is chronic. How sterile, I think, this unease is felt by all, while absurd suffering is individual.

My fishbowl-body, lazy-body, becomes endless as it consumes itself, I think. Unproductive waiting for views of sunset in your neighborhood. Mauve spilling on still humid eyes, all the intense blue turned into premature night.

I could not see who was who well. The next minute I was on the ground, with my legs held by one of them. I managed to keep up the struggle with great difficulty, my throat ripping apart with silent screams. I tried to look where B might be, but they had my head trapped between two arms that my hands were scratching and tearing at as much as possible— at the skin, the cloth, anything within reach. Within this frozen mobility, I could only hear B's drowned breathing.

No use hoping to hear another sound, her voice made no more sound, disappeared from my ears just as all of her disappeared from my sight. Almost immobile, I felt that they took off my sandals and threw them to the other side of the street. I was never in such an impassive neighborhood. The houses seemed to have been swallowed by the night, holograms substituting for the real ones, the ones that might have been there, at some point, some time. All the windows darkened, no one there had the capacity to come out, to at least look, the whole world appeared to have fallen into the most lethargic of sleeps.

I could not imagine B on top of the hood, with the bald guy on top, or anyone else, I did not want to, despite the sounds, the noisy evidence of the metal, of everyone's screams. I wished I had been more alone than ever, that it was me under the most disgusting guy, that it was me bursting into that sort of muffled, horrible tremor, that tragic, mimic's shake.

I wished I had dreamed it, had been able to predict it, had been far and alert, conscious of the inevitable. To be the most skeptical, the most distrusting, the strongest in the world. In some way to have had the opportunity to be prepared, to anticipate the scene, to take a lot of time digesting the most remote possibility, and taking it as a given.

To stomp on even a minimal comparison of statistics, any trust at all on luck eternal. All of the women, the same ones, again and again, subjected to the same violence the same nights, all of them. The ideas were lost like the passive breathing of B, like my hysterical, repressed screams, my attempts to bite the hand that covered my mouth.

How not to sense any groan, any sign of anything. In less than one minute I learned to hold in a strange rage, an unknown fury, some destructive desires. I learned hatred.

If I could have made the least little movement, I would have bashed in the head of that guy with my hands, that guy who probably would have sat two desks away from mine in secondary school, who would have sold me an ice cream last week, who would have been a stretcher-bearer in the hospital where my grandmother died.

The only area that my eyes could see was the part under the car, the red strip that hung from the exhaust and B's feet, her nails also red. The worst torture was the impotence, the bewildering submission, like in a nightmare, the immediate hopelessness. The turtle trying to go faster while the hare stopped to eat. Lost cause.

Maybe three real minutes had passed, all the time in the world, all the time of a human life, when the first police car illuminated the street with its high beams.

It turned the corner without giving them time to react. Someone probably, after all, had dared to call, to accept just a bit of responsibility amid the silent death of the neighborhood. The profound relief slowly drowned the profound anger. As soon as I felt free I ran to B, knocked down, abandoned by the guy who already had police on top of him when he tried to run.

He released her and B collapsed, fainted, lifeless. On the blacktop she looked like a broken, battered dummy.

One policeman approached. He tried to put me at ease and bother me with stupid questions. He was about 40 and had serious, almost sad eyes. He tried to separate me from B when he saw how badly she was breathing, her translucent skin, but I could not let her go. He left us like that and returned to the patrol car in front of the Nissan. B seemed to revive, saw my feet and held more tightly to me. I could feel her perfectly measured heartbeat, breathe on her rhythm, nervous but gentle. I grew happy, above all else, that she was so dichotomous in the worst of circumstances.

I saw that she wasn't more fragile than me, maybe my strength was even less. Another police car arrived in two minutes to pick us up, and we learned they had not captured everyone, that they didn't know how many there were.

We filled out the complaint at the police station on Zapata, very quickly, without hesitation, without thinking about anything, without considering the danger of those guys on the loose, that they could recognize us at some point, that they would be watching us, without feeling more free than before, without shrinking our burden, more like with something of death. So many others. All of them. Out there. Day after day.

The warmth of B's hand in mine was more than I could have hoped for at the end of the night, at the end of the fear. That warmth was not at all fictional, it was a warmth that healed, comforted, reconciliated with all things.

We never spoke of that night, never wrote that final period, never closed anything. I think we preferred to wait for a pending conclusion, a time that would be perfect, impossible. I never told B about the sensual sound of the Chinese flute, or the red strip.

Almost at the end we realized how totally absurd it would be to think again about a past that could dissolve itself into memory, like a lie never uttered, or never revealed. The invention of a paranoid mind. Nothing more.

"Let's see. Make a "u" with your lips and say "e", that is the "i-grek", the Greek "y", that is how you pronounce the "u" in tortue... Turtulutú-chapeau-pointu ! Repite avec moi..."

It smells good, your hair.

"Dis tortue, dors-tu nue ? Say turtle. Do you sleep naked? Say turtle, you sleep naked..."

"Ok, stop. Tell me, do you sleep naked?"

The Writers

Jorge Alberto Aguiar Díaz (JAAD)

Jorge Alberto Aguiar Díaz is a fiction writer, poet, and literature workshop leader. In 2002 he published his short story collection *Adiós a las Almas* (Letras Cubanas). His opinion columns appear on *CubaNet* and he is the webmaster of the blogs *Fogonero Emergente* and *Cuarto de Máquinas/Compasión por Cuba*. He was also the editor-in-chief of the digital independent literary and opinion magazine *Cacharro(s)*. He temporarily lives in Spain, as a Tibetan Buddhist monk.

Lien Carrazana Lau

Lien Carrazana Lau is a fiction writer, digital editor, painter, graphic designer, and the webmaster of *Liencarrazana.com* and *La China Fuera de la Caja*. Her first narrative volume, *Faithless* (Habitación 69, México DF), was published in 2011, and her stories have been included in anthologies, such as *Vida laboral y otros minicuentos* (Caja China, 2006), and in the literary magazine *El Cuentero*. She is also a staff member of the opinion, literary, and news website *Diario de Cuba*. She temporarily lives in Madrid and holds a B.S. from the San Alejandro Fine Arts Academy, Havana.

Gleyvis Coro Montanet

Gleyvis Coro Montanet has published the poetry collections *Escribir en la piedra* (Loynaz, 2000), *Poemas Briosos* (Aristas de Cobre, Córdoba, España, 2003), *Aguardando al guardabosque* (Loynaz, 2006), and *Jaulas* (Letras Cubanas, 2009). She has also published a volume of short-fiction, *Con los pies en las nubes* (Vitral, 1998), and the novel *La burbuja* (Unión, 2007).

Ahmel Echevarría Peré

Ahmel Echevarría Peré is a fiction writer, photographer, editor, and the webmaster of *Vercuba* and *Centronelio*. He holds a B.S. degree in Mechanical Engineering from ISPJAE University, Havana. He has published the narrative books *Esquirlas* (Letras Cubanas, 2006), *Inventario* (Unión, 2007), and *Días de Entrenamiento* (FRA, Prague, Czech Republic, 2012). He has also been included in several Cuban literary anthologies, such as: *Los Que Cuentan* (Cajachina, 2007), *La Ínsula Fabulante: El Cuento Cubano en la Revolución 1959-2008* (Letras Cubanas, 2008), and *La Fiamma in Bocca: Giovanni Narratori Cubani* (Voland, 2009). His novels *Pastel Para Pitbulls*, *La Noria*, and *Búfalos Camino al Matadero* are to be published in Cuba this year.

As a columnist he has collaborated with the independent digital magazine *Voces*, *Diario de Cuba*, *The Revolution Evening Post*, and the dialogue section of the Hermanos Saíz Association. He lives in Havana.

Michel Encinosa Fú

Michel Encinosa Fú is a fiction writer and editor who holds a B.S. degree in English Language and Literature. He has published *Sol negro* (Extramuros, 2001), *Niños de neón* (Letras Cubanas, 2001), *Veredas* (Extramuros, 2006), *Dioses de neón* (Letras Cubanas, 2006), *Dopamina, sans amour* (Abril, 2008), *Enemigo sin voz* (Abril, 2008), *El Cadillac rojo y la gran mentira* (Loynaz, 2009), *Casi la verdad* (Matanzas, 2009), *Todos tenemos un mal día* (Loynaz, 2009), and *Vivir y morir sin ángeles* (Unión, 2009). In addition, he has been included in more than twenty anthologies in Cuba as well as in Italy, Spain, Brazil, Argentina, Mexico, and the United States.

Jhortensia Espineta Osuna

Jhortensia Espineta Osuna is a fiction writer, poet, and cultural promoter who has published the short story collection *Zona de Exorcismo* (Ácana, 2006). Her texts have also appeared in the Cuban literary magazines *Antenas* and *El Caimán Barbudo*. She holds a B.S. from the National Art School, E.N.A., Havana, and lives in Camagüey, Cuba.

Carlos Esquivel

Carlos Esquivel has published numerous poetry collections: *Perros ladrándole a Dios* (1999), *Balada de los perros oscuros* (2001), *Tren de Oriente* (2001), *El boulevard de los Capuchinos* (2003), *Bala de cañón* (2006), *Matando a los pieles rojas* (2008), *Los hijos del kamikaze* (2008), and *Los ciclos de nadie* (2013). Additionally, Esquivel has written several books of fiction: *Los animales del cuerpo* (2001), *Una ventana al cielo* (2002), *La isla imposible y otras mujeres* (2002), and *Un lobo, una colina* (2011).

Abel Fernández-Larrea

Abel Fernández-Larrea is a fiction writer, editor, translator, essayist, musician, and university professor who has published the book *Absolut Röntgen* (Caja China, 2009). His novel *1991* remains unpublished, although it was awarded the Frónesis (2012) Creative Writing Grant from the Hermanos Saíz Association, Cuba.

In 2012 he also won the Matanzas City Foundation Award for his short-story collection *Berlineses*.

His stories and essays have appeared in Cuban literary magazines, including *Matanzas*, *El Cuentero*, *La Letra del Escriba*, *El Caimán Barbudo*, and *Voces*. He works as an editor for the University of Havana's publishing house and lives in Havana, Cuba.

Raúl Flores

Raúl Flores writes in Spanish and English, and has received most of Cuba's national literary awards and creative writing grants. In Cuba, he has published *El lado oscuro de la luna* (Extramuros, 2000), *El hombre que vendió el mundo* (Letras Cubanas, 2001), *Bronceado de luna* (Extramuros, 2003), *Días de lluvia* (Unicornio, 2004), *Rayo de luz* (Abril, 2005), *Balada de Jeanette* (Loynaz, 2007), *La carne luminosa de los gigantes* (Abril, 2008), and *Paperback writer* (Matanzas, 2010).

His short-stories and literary critiques have been published in magazines and anthologies from Cuba, Spain, the United States, the Dominican Republic, Italy, Mexico, and Brazil. He was also the head of the digital literary magazine, *33 y un tercio*, an independent project that released 14 editions from 2004 to 2012. As a cultural promoter, from 2004 to 2008, he managed Polaroid Space, a venue for underground music, audiovisuals, performances, and readings that took place in the heart of El Vedado, Havana. He is a member of the National Union of Cuban Writers and Artists (UNEAC) and is currently writing two books: *Ella quería ser escritora* and *La chica más hermosa del mundo*.

Jorge Enrique Lage

Jorge Enrique Lage is editor of the magazine *El cuentero* and the publishing house Caja China, of the Onelio Jorge Cardoso Literary Training Center. He has published the short story collections *Yo fui un adolescente ladrón de tumbas* (Extramuros, 2004), *Fragmentos encontrados en La Rampa* (Abril, 2004), *Los ojos de fuego verde* (Abril, 2005), *El color de la sangre diluida* (Letras Cubanas, 2007), *Vultureffect* (Unión, 2011), and the novel *Carbono 14, una novela de culto* (Altazor, Perú, 2010). In addition, Lage is a professional biochemist.

Polina Martínez Shviétsova

Polina Martínez Shviétsova is a fiction writer, poet, performer, and freelance journalist who graduated as a Library Technician in 1999. Martínez has published two poetry collections in Cuba, *Gotas de fuego* (2004) and *Tao del azar* (2005), as well as the fiction volume *Hechos con Metallica* (2008). She has participated in a research panel on Russian literature in Cuban culture (2010), and her essay "Borsch no liga con Ajiaco" appears in the book *Caviar with Rum; Cuba-USSR and the Post-Soviet Experience* (Palgrave Macmillian, New York, 2012). She is a columnist for the websites *Cuba Encuentro, Diario de Cuba,* and *CubaNet*. She lives in Havana.

Lizabel Mónica

Lizabel Mónica is a fiction writer, poet, art critic, and editor. She is the coordinator of the multifaceted international art and writing project *Desliz*, as well as the *Desliz* digital magazine. She has probably edited more blogs than anyone else in Cuba, including *Cuba Fake News*, *Paladeo in Deleite*, *Revista Desliz*, *Broken Spanglish*, *Lizabel Mónica*, and *La Taza de Café*. She holds a B.S. in History and is currently studying for a PhD at Princeton University.

Osdany Morales

Osdany Morales has published the short story collections *Minuciosas puertas estrechas* (Unión, 2007) and *Papyrus* (Letras Cubanas, 2011; Sudaquia, New York, 2012). His texts have also been included in several anthologies of new Cuban literature, such as *Maneras de narrar* (Unión, 2006), *Los que cuentan* (Caja China, 2008), and *La fiamma in boca* (Voland, Italia, 2009), as well as in a number of magazines such as *El Cuentero* (Cuba), *El perro* (Mexico), *Quimera* (Spain), and *Ragazine.cc* (USA). He currently lives in Brooklyn and, thanks to a fellowship awarded by Banco Santander, has received an MFA in Creative Writing at New York University, where he is now a PhD candidate in Latin American Literature.

Erick Mota

Erick Mota has published the fiction books *Bajo Presión* (Gente Nueva, 2008), *Algunos recuerdos que valen la pena* (Abril, 2010), *La Habana Underguater* (Atom Press, 2010), and *Ojos de cesio radiactivo* (Red Ediciones SL, 2012).

Orlando Luis Pardo Lazo

Orlando Luis Pardo Lazo has edited the cultural magazine *Extramuros*, as well as several independent Cuban digital magazines: *Cacharro(s)*, *The Revolution Evening Post*, and *Voces*. He is the webmaster of the opinion blog *Lunes De Post-Revolución* and the photoblog *Boring Home Utopics*. He lives in Havana and temporarily resides in the United States where, from Pittsburgh, he has compiled this exclusive collection of new Cuban narratives for *Sampsonia Way Magazine*. He also holds a B.S. in Biochemistry.

Lia Villares

Lia Villares is a fiction writer, musician, blogger, and visual artist. She hasn't yet published any books. Her stories have appeared in national magazines and anthologies, but most of her creativity goes into the digital world, where she is one of the most important social activists of the Cuban blogosphere. She blogs at *Hechizamiento Habanémico Hebdomadario*.

The Translators

Diana Álvarez-Amell, María Lourdes Capote, Karen González, David Iaconangelo, Alison Macomber, Guillermo Parra, Mary Jo Porter, Zachary A. Tackett, and Juan O. Tamayo generously volunteered their time and abilities to translate *Generation Zero* into English. Some of these translators have had their work appear in publications such as *Words Without Borders*, *Typo Magazine*, and the *Huffington Post*.

The Artists

Danilo Maldonado Machado, EL SEXTO
(Cover artwork)
El Sexto is currently one of the most persecuted Cuban artists. The political police have arrested him multiple times, invaded his home, and seized his artwork and cans of spray paint without any legal order and without filing charges. On more than one occasion officers have forcibly removed t-shirts of his own design, which honored Cuban political martyrs Laura Pollán and Oswaldo Payá, from his body. In response, El Sexto tattooed Pollán and Payá's images on his skin so that no one could erase them. He is committed to "bad-painting" and to the many technical innovations he thinks up. He loves throwing flyers out to crowds, as well as modifying the Revolutionary slogans on official posters and traffic signs. He lives in Havana. Personal exhibits: *No son Cinco (They aren't Five)*, Havana, 2011; *Dos456 Space*, Havana, 2012 (Closed by the political police at its opening); *Este año quemaré dos muñecos viejos (This year two old dolls will burn up)*, Havana, 2012; *Cinco años de vida artística / arte inútil. (Five years of artistic life / useless art)*, Havana, 2013.

Luis Trápaga *(Back cover artwork)*
Luis Trápaga is a painter and writer who studied at the San Alejandro Fine Arts Academy. He has worked as an art designer and film director for the Cuban Institute for Cinema Art and Industry's (ICAIC) animation studio. His artwork has been published in national magazines, such as *La Gaceta de Cuba* and on the cover of the collection *Pinos Nuevos Prize* (Letras Cubanas). He also joined the community art project of Baconao Park, Santiago de Cuba, and collaborated on the restoration of La Merced Church of Old Havana, a Cuban national patrimony. He lives in Havana City. Personal Exhibits: *Dos caminos (Two Ways)*, International Press Center, Habana, 2001; *Figuraciones y Desfiguraciones (Imaginations and Disfigurements)*, National Medical Library, La Habana, 2002; *En el medio... (In the Middle)*, Juan David Gallery, Cinema Yara Cultural Center, La Habana, 2002; *Abstracciones (Abstractions)*, Horizontes Caribbean Hotel, La Habana 2002.

Sampsonia Way Magazine

SampsoniaWay.org is an online magazine with interviews, columns, literary excerpts, essays, and multi-media features by writers from around the world, along with daily coverage of global threats to writers. *Generation Zero/Cuba* is the first in our series of anthologies of literature from countries where writers and free speech have been threatened. *SampsoniaWay.org* is published by City of Asylum/Pittsburgh.

City of Asylum/Pittsburgh

City of Asylum/Pittsburgh provides long-term sanctuary to endangered literary writers, along with a broad range of residencies and programs in a community setting to encourage cross-cultural exchange. We also anchor neighborhood economic development by transforming blighted properties into homes for our programs and energizing public spaces through public art with text-based components.

Made in the USA
Lexington, KY
26 January 2014